Homicide at the Holidays

Saltcliff Mysteries
Book 3

Nancy Stewart

Chapter One

"Are you ready?" My niece Diantha's voice came from around the corner. She was waiting out of view of the kitchen, where I was elbows-deep in Christmas baking.

"As ready as I'm going to be with my hands covered with flour," I laughed.

Taco Dog was curled on his bed in the corner, and though his ears pricked at Diantha's voice—they were best friends, after all—he was deep into a midday nap. It would take the promise of food to rouse him at this point.

"Close your eyes," Diantha called.

"Okay. Closed." I did as I was told and waited next to the far counter, my fruitcake batter waiting to one side and the dinner roll dough I'd been kneading spread on the board behind me. I held my hands out like a surgeon would, careful not to get flour on anything I'd just have to clean later.

"Ta da!" Diantha cried out, and I heard her leap into the kitchen.

"Does that mean I can look now?"

"Yes! Ta da was the grand reveal. You were supposed to open your eyes when I said that."

"Sorry. Wasn't quite clear," I said, opening my eyes. Diantha stood before me with a red and green scarf wrapped around her neck and draped down her front. "Oh Danny, that is really beautiful! You've mastered it!"

My niece glowed beneath my praise, but her lips puckered, and she shrugged. "I've mastered the double crochet in completely straight lines."

I shook my head. "Between this and the dog leashes you've been selling in town, you've mastered quite a lot." Diantha's colorful leashes were a hit over at the Mutt Modiste, and she had a steady business going at this point. Now she'd begun learning to make things she could wear and use at home. One of my favorite things was sitting with my niece and working new stitches, watching her eyes light up as she grasped how each one added to the overall pattern as we made something new.

"Thanks, Aunt Dolly." Diantha grinned. "I'm going to give it to Amal for Christmas."

"She will love that." I knew our friend and the inn's

manager, Amal, would be touched by Diantha's gift. "Want to help with some baking? I'm way behind."

"I could do those candy cane cookies Mom used to like. The ones with two colors of dough twisted together?"

"That would be great," I told her. "I've been focused on getting the yeast doughs together and haven't gotten nearly enough sweets done." I glanced over my shoulder at the kitchen table, where multiple tins of holiday sweets were stacked in preparation for the week ahead.

"When do they get here?" Diantha asked as she bent down to pull a mixing bowl from the cabinet below the counter.

"They'll begin arriving this afternoon," I said. "I think the whole family should be here by late tonight, assuming this storm doesn't impede travel."

My niece paused and tilted her head. "Aunt Dolly, I've lived here my whole life, and never once has it ever snowed. The forecast is wrong. The weather guy must be on something."

I raised an eyebrow at the suggestion, but hoped she was right. "There are a few of them who all seem to agree about this one."

"We just don't get white Christmas on the California coast," Diantha sighed. "Never have, never will. But I wish we did. I've only seen snow once!"

"Well, I saw plenty when I lived in Virginia, and it makes quite a mess of things. I really hope you're right. It's the last thing we need this week." The entire inn was booked by one family, and I'd gotten the distinct impression that they had very high expectations for us to deliver the perfect holiday. A freak snowstorm would not help.

"Knock knock!" Amal's voice came from the living room, where a big wooden door separated the apartment I shared with my niece from the lobby of the Saltcliff Bed and Breakfast.

"We're in the kitchen, Amal!" I called back.

Diantha's eyes widened as she looked toward the door where Amal was approaching. She whipped off the scarf and tucked it into a kitchen drawer.

"Oh, I could have guessed you were in here based on the smell alone," she said, coming in to join us. "Dahlia, are you going overboard?"

"I don't think so," I told her. "I want to make sure we don't run out of anything and that everything is just perfect."

I'd shopped several times to stock up for the week. It was unusual, but for this week, we were serving lunches and dinners on several days in addition to the usual breakfast. That had required plugging in the second big refrigerator we kept down in the basement, which was now completely full of turkey and all the fixings. Every time I went down there to put something in or take something out of the refrigerator, I was startled by noises coming from the other side of the basement, where the old speakeasy we'd discovered was being renovated for the new year. The work was well underway, though it was set to pause for the week of the holiday.

"I think the Donovans will be impressed, if the baked goods are anything to go on," Amal said, picking up a coconut macaroon from the tray on the table and popping it into her mouth. "Delicious."

"What's their deal again?" Diantha asked over her shoulder as she cracked eggs into the bowl in front of her.

"Their 'deal,'" Amal laughed, "is that the Donovan family built the Saltcliff Bed and Breakfast originally. Daisy bought the property from the woman who is bringing her whole family this week, Margaret Donovan. She is the granddaughter of the original owner."

"That's so crazy," Diantha said.

I stifled a sigh at the mention of my sister. Since I'd discovered her last letter to me, the pain I'd held at her absence from my life over the last years had softened into a deep sadness at her absence from life in general. Especially at the holiday, I missed my twin sister.

"It is kind of crazy," Amal continued. "And I believe Margaret Donovan might have even lived here at one point in her life."

It was hard to imagine. I thought of this place as Daisy's, but when my sister died and left the inn to her daughter—with me as guardian of both the inn and my niece until Diantha was of age—I had begun to think of it as a symbol of our family. It was odd to hear that it had significance to some other family. Still, I hoped there would be some interesting history that I might glean from the Donovan family about the inn I had come to love.

"And what do you think about the odds for this snowstorm to materialize?" I asked my friend and coworker.

"Not a chance," Amal laughed. "It just doesn't snow here. Rain? Definitely."

"So more wet Christmas than white Christmas?"

"Yep." Amal grinned and turned back toward the door. "I'll be out front in case anyone arrives early, but the place is spotless. Every room is pristine. Let me know if you need any help with anything."

We'd kept the inn clear for the two nights leading up to the arrival of the Donovan family, wanting to get everything prepared perfectly for them. Since they'd be taking every room in the inn except one, it was going to be a very different experience than when we had lots of different guests in residence. I was looking forward to it, but I was also a little bit nervous. Innkeeping—and parenting—were both very new to me.

I set the rolls to rise, finished putting the fruitcake in to bake, and helped Diantha color the dough for her candy cane cookies, and then I washed my hands and headed out to the lobby.

I was just stepping through the door, Taco on my heels,

when Zeke, the manager of the construction crew downstairs, stepped into the lobby from the hallway.

"Ms. Vale," he boomed, giving me the grin that seemed to always occupy his ruddy-cheeked face. "Things are looking good down in the basement bar, you wanna come see?"

"Are you finishing up for the week?" I asked.

"Yep, just wanted to get your go-ahead to send the guys home."

"I'll come take a look," I said. "Be right back," I said to Amal, who was busily typing something behind the reception desk. She shot me a smile and then focused again on the screen in front of her.

I followed Zeke down the hall, and through the door that led to the basement laundry and storage room and the speakeasy. I'd discovered the hidden door to the secret space a few months earlier, and while we'd decided to keep the door functional, it would be concealed from those inside the bar, just as it had been in the twenties. The bar's entrance would be around the back of the inn. Where once there'd been a non-descript and somewhat hidden entrance to the club, now there would be a sign and we hoped it would do a good business and help us contribute to the inn's bottom line.

We stepped through the door, and I marveled at how much had been done. The walls had been stripped and refinished, the burnished wood gleaming under a new coat of glaze. The bar itself had been refurbished, and we'd added a wall of copper tile behind it, to evoke the gilded feel of the era. The ceiling was pressed copper, and gave the entire space a cozy, hidden-away vibe. It was perfect. The old, wide-planked flooring was still coated with dust, but until everything else was done, that would wait.

"I just wanted to show you a couple things," Zeke said. He stepped behind the bar and indicated a new panel of switches. "The wiring is just about done here. We'll get the new sconces put on and finish the chandelier after the holidays."

"Sounds good," I said, glancing up at the magnificent chandelier we'd decided to freshen up and keep.

"And you sure you want to keep this bookcase functional? You might end up getting visitors you don't want upstairs." Zeke motioned to the bookcase that swung into a hidden passage that led to a stairway connecting to one of the upstairs guest rooms.

"I want to keep it, but maybe we could fashion some kind of lock?"

Zeke nodded. "I'll have a think on what would work and stay true to the rest of the decor."

"Perfect."

"What do you want to do with the kegs back here?" He pulled the bookcase open, and we stepped into the small, dark space on the other side. There was a recessed area where two kegs sat, coated with a thick layer of dust.

"I don't know," I said. I'd ignored them until now, but it made sense to get them moved out. "Any idea what's in them?"

Zeke shook his head. "Didn't want to disturb your things."

I looked at him, pleased with the man's sense of etiquette and politeness. "That was nice of you. Still, maybe we should pull them out and see what's inside at least?"

"Sure," Zeke said. He bent down and wrapped his beefy arms around one of the barrels, pulling it out into the open space. I moved out of his way, allowing him to scoot it into the better-lit area in the bar.

"Lemme just get this other one." He repeated the process with the second barrel, and for a moment we both just looked at them.

"Alcohol, you think?" I asked, thinking of the history of the space we were in. If it had been a hidden bar during the Prohibition era, that would make sense to me.

"Most likely," Zeke said. "Wonder if it wouldn't be dried out by now, a century later."

I watched as the man retrieved a pry bar from a box of tools next to the wall and went to work on the top of one barrel. After a few minutes, and a loud crack, he pried the top up, giving us a view inside.

"Think you're right, Ms. Vale. Liquid in there, way down at the bottom."

There was, indeed, some murky liquid sloshing around in the depths of the barrel's interior. It gave off a faint smell, but nothing I could identify.

"Probably the same in this other one," Zeke said, going to work on the second barrel.

As he pried up the lid, the smell that came out was distinctly different, a mix of strong liquor and something else, something far more pungent, even though it was faint.

"Uh, Ms. Vale..." Zeke was peering into the barrel and as I stared at him, the color drained from his usually red face. "This isn't old liquor."

"What is it?" I asked, dread pooling in my stomach.

"I'm no expert, but I think there's a body in here."

Chapter Two

"Did you say..."

"A body, yeah," Zeke confirmed wrinkling his big nose as he straightened and looked up at me, his eyebrows coming together like caterpillars trying to hug each other. "Wanna take a look?"

Oddly, I did. Maybe it was that it was tough to believe there was actually a body here at the inn, or perhaps it was just my generally curious and logical nature. I liked to see things for myself to truly understand them. Trust, but verify, as they say.

I nodded and stepped closer to the huge man, who wrenched the lid of the keg up once more for me to peer beneath. It was dark, and the smell was noticeably less enjoyable at close range, but there was no question that what I saw within was a body.

As I stepped back, Zeke let the lid drop again. "What should we do now?" he asked.

I looked between him and the barrel, which sat in the center of my new speakeasy. "I guess for now, we call the police. I think this place just became a crime scene."

He nodded, his eyes widening. "Should I tell the guys they can take off for the holiday?"

"Yes," I said. "And please don't mention the, ah…"

"The body in the barrel. Sure thing, Ms. Vale." He wrung his gigantic hands in front of him, stepped away to collect his toolbox, and then moved near again, frowning at me as I stood next to the barrel. "I don't feel right leaving you down here alone."

Zeke was trying to be a gentleman, I realized. "Thank you, Zeke. I'll go up with you." Though I followed the big man back to the lobby, it wasn't as if I hadn't been alone with this body several times before. I just hadn't realized it. Still, the speakeasy did have a whole different atmosphere now that I knew what was inside the barrels.

In the lobby, Zeke turned back to me. "The guys are all around the back. I'll let them know we're off for the week now and make sure the back door is locked." He looked uncertainly between Amal and me. "You ladies have a wonderful holiday."

"You too, Zeke," Amal said cheerfully.

"Think you'll need me to talk to anyone about the…" Zeke waved a hand toward the back hallway.

"I'll ask Detective Sanderson. He'll be in touch, I'm sure," I told him.

Zeke headed out the front door and I turned to face Amal, whose mouth had formed into a stiff line.

"What was Zeke gesturing to that will require us to call Owen in his formal capacity as Detective Sanderson?" Amal asked, her words slow and full of dread.

"Well," I said, considering how to phrase this. It wasn't as if there was a body sprawled on the floor downstairs. It was tucked neatly into a barrel, where it had been tidily hidden for who knew how long. "There's something down-stairs that Owen probably needs to look at."

"Something or someone?" Amal knew that the last few times I'd had to call the detective in an official capacity, there'd been a murder involved.

"Someone," I said. "But nothing to get upset about. Whoever it is, they've been down there a long, long time."

"Oh, that makes it so much better," Amal said, waving a hand at me.

"It does, doesn't it?" I was glad she agreed.

"No, Dahlia. I'm being sarcastic. Is there a dead body in our basement?" She nearly shrieked this last part, rousing Taco from his slumber on his dog bed next to the door between the inn and the apartment. He watched us curiously.

"Yes, there is a dead body in the basement."

As I delivered this sentence—somewhat redundantly, I

thought—the front door of the inn swung open and an elegant woman stepped in, followed by a second, younger woman, a man, and a teenaged girl who looked just a little older than Diantha.

"Did you say a dead body?" The man asked, offering no preamble whatsoever.

Amal rushed out from behind the desk, clasping her hands at her chest and wearing a grin I would have categorized as maniacal. "No, no, of course not! We were discussing whether you might like a red TODDY when you arrive, and now, here you are!"

Amal's excitement completely roused Taco, who leaped to his feet and charged toward the group, but I caught his collar and coaxed him into a sit before he managed to bowl anyone over.

The small group stared at Amal, who was standing before them, practically vibrating with energy and still wearing the fearsome smile.

"You are the Donovans?" I asked.

"We are," the older woman agreed, moving her bright gaze from Amal to me and Taco. "Are you Dahlia Vale?"

"I am. And this is Amal Sharma, the manager of the Saltcliff Bed and Breakfast. And this is my service dog, Taco."

The woman smiled at Taco, but said nothing, her head swiveling slowly around the expansive lobby. I had a feeling she missed very little with those shrewd eyes.

"Well," the man said. "I'm Peter. This is my mother Margaret Donovan, my wife Sabrina, and my daughter Isabelle."

"It's lovely to meet you." Amal seemed to have regained her usual composure and extended a hand to shake with Peter.

"Come on in," I suggested, moving the group away from the door. "You're welcome to leave your luggage there for the moment while we get rooms sorted."

Taco moved at my side, pretending for the moment to be exceptionally well-behaved, which I appreciated.

"Can I pet your dog?" Isabelle asked, stretching out a hand.

"Of course," I told her. "He would love that."

A moment later, Taco was on his back, Isabelle rubbing his belly as he sprawled on the floor, and she knelt next to him.

"And that toddy you mentioned?" Sabrina said with a smile. "Although, I wouldn't need mine to be red, I don't think."

"Coming right up," I said, exchanging a look with Amal. Toddies were not part of the plan, and now I needed to slip away to investigate how to make one and see if we even had the ingredients for such a thing. "I'll leave out the red dye. It was just an idea. Festive, you know. Be right back. Amal, can you please check the Donovans in?"

"Of course!" Amal headed back behind the desk, while

the Donovans spread out around the lobby, which was decorated with twinkling lights, garlands that emanated the scent of pine and cinnamon, and a massive glittering tree in front of the windows that looked out to the back deck and the Pacific Ocean beyond.

I slipped back into the apartment, pulling my phone from my pocket. It might have been prudent to call Owen first, but I felt like the family out front was the more timely concern. After all, the body in the basement had been there for years already. What was another hour?

Toddies, as it turned out, were not a heavy lift in terms of ingredients. I joined Diantha back in the kitchen. "The Donovans have started to arrive," I told her.

"Yay!" Diantha bounced on her toes and clapped her hands, the movement reminding me so much of my happy-go-lucky sister that it took the wind out of me for a moment. Then she turned back to the frosting she was beating, and the image of Daisy was gone.

I mixed up the whiskey, lemon, hot water, and honey, and poured it into a serving pitcher, which I set on a tray with six glass mugs. I shaved a curl of lemon rind into each and then headed back out to the lobby.

"Oh, that looks lovely," Sabrina said eagerly as I set the toddies on the sideboard next to the rum cake and Madeline cookies I'd put out that morning.

"Get me one, will you, honey?" Peter called from the desk where he seemed to have taken charge of check in.

"I'll have one too," Margaret said from where she stood in front of one of the bookcases in the corner we referred to as the library. There were floor-to-ceiling bookcases stuffed with books I still hadn't properly investigated. Perhaps they'd been here as long as the inn had. Or as long as the body in the basement?

"Mom, maybe you should wait," Peter said in a scolding tone. "You know how alcohol affects you."

Peter turned back to the reception desk, so he didn't see the searing look that Margaret shot his way, but the older woman moved gracefully to where I stood and extended a hand for a glass. "Thank you," she said with a smile as I handed one to her.

"Of course," I said. I carried a third glass to Peter, who was quizzing Amal about the incoming storm.

"I doubt very much it will be as bad as they're saying," she assured him. "I've lived in Saltcliff for two decades, and I've seen snow here once. And it was much more of a novelty than an issue."

"That's what we like to hear," Peter said, picking up the mug I'd offered and lifting it to his lips. "Delicious," he boomed, smiling at me over the rim.

"Good," I said, relieved that the first check in seemed to be going smoothly. We hoped to impress the Donovans and earn their endorsement going forward. Having the original family's blessing would help business at the inn in the future.

"We'll take your bags up if you just let us know whose is whose," Amal said to Peter, who was gazing around the lobby with a smile on his face.

"These are mine," Isabelle said, stepping close to a bright yellow hardback suitcase and a pink backpack. "But I can carry them."

"Your room is called 'Alice,'" Peter told her, handing her a brass key. We hadn't switched the doors to electronic locks, though it was in the plans for the future. I thought the old brass keys had a certain charm.

"Alice? My room has a name?"

"For *Alice in Wonderland*," I explained. "All the rooms are named for my sister Daisy's favorite literary characters. Yours is on the second floor. Down the hall on the left."

Isabelle grinned and picked up her bags. "I've never had my own room before!"

"Well, we're right next door, so don't get any ideas," Peter said.

"I love the literary theme," Margaret commented. "When my father ran the inn, we simply numbered the rooms."

I smiled at her, knowing Daisy would have loved her appreciation.

"I'll take your things to the Gandalf," Amal told him. "And Margaret is in the Jane Eyre Suite on the first floor."

"I'll just take your bags into your room," I told Margaret. "And will be right back."

I wheeled Margaret's large suitcase to the suite and set it on the luggage rack inside after a quick glance around to make sure everything was perfect. There was a garland across the mantle of the fireplace, which glowed merrily with a low gas flame. A tiny tree sat in one corner, decorated in silver and platinum blue, and the tea service was ready on the top of the dresser, complete with peppermint sticks and white chocolate stir spoons for hot chocolate.

As I hurried back to the lobby, intent on finally contacting Owen, Margaret called to me.

"Dahlia dear, do come sit with me a moment."

"Mother, I'm sure she has things to do," Peter told her. I was beginning to understand some of the family dynamic, I thought. Especially when Margaret waved away his words and patted the spot next to her on the couch.

Isabelle had returned and was happily sipping hot chocolate and stroking Taco, who'd laid his head across her lap.

Sabrina had disappeared upstairs to her room, and Peter was milling around, investigating items in the lobby shelves.

"I have time," I assured the woman, taking a seat at her side.

"So, I'm sure you know this inn was built by my grandfather, George, in 1920."

I nodded, leaning forward a little, enthralled. I'd hoped to learn a bit more about the inn's history.

"And my father Henry inherited it when his father died." A little smile crossed Margaret's lips. "Did you know I grew up here? In the rooms you live in now, I would guess."

"I suspected," I told her. "I hope you're pleased with the way the inn has been maintained. My sister owned it first and I know she worked hard to keep a lot of the original charm."

Margaret smiled. "Of course she did. You've all done a lovely job," she said. "I wonder if at some point it might not be too much trouble to visit the apartment?"

I hadn't exactly cleaned the apartment to be guest-ready. "Sure, maybe a bit later in the visit? Let me get it tidied up first?"

"Oh, of course, I don't want to be a bother," Margaret said.

Peter made a hissing noise of annoyance from where he stood nearby, pretending not to be listening.

Margaret and I sat quietly for a moment, my phone heavy against my hip where it rested in my pocket. I really needed to call Owen, but then Margaret began speaking again.

"This is an old Saltcliff heirloom, in fact," Margaret said, extracting a gold pocket watch from her purse. "I thought it would be nice to show the family since we'd be back here. It has a long history. I'm not sure who it belonged to originally, but I believe it was my grandfather's."

"Ooh," Isabelle said, rising to come inspect the shining golden watch. She reached out and Margaret placed it into her hands. The girl inspected the bright bauble, and I finally gave into the pressure of needing to make a call.

"Please excuse me for a moment, I just need to attend to something," I said.

"Of course, of course," Margaret said, reaching forward and picking up her hot toddy glass again as a smile settled on her lips and her eyes moved softly around the room.

I slipped through the apartment door and pulled my phone from my pocket.

Chapter Three

I stared at the phone in my hand for a beat.

It was the holidays. I knew Owen had family in town—his sister Elsa and his dad, Gary. I knew that because Owen and I had dinner a few nights earlier, and he'd told me his plans.

He was technically not working... but he was also the only detective in the Saltcliff Police Department and the only one I knew personally. And he was maybe, kind of, my boyfriend.

I decided on a text. Less intrusive, less assumptive. He could read it at his convenience.

Of course, a body kind of suggested urgency... but a decades-old body? Maybe less urgency?

I typed out a text, working hard to achieve the right balance between potential homicide and holiday cheer.

> Me: Hello! Hope your week is off to a
> good start. Our holiday guests have
> begun to arrive, so things are good here.
> There is one little thing I'd love to chat
> with you about when you have a
> moment. Not urgent. Or maybe kind of
> urgent. But not horribly urgent… How is
> your family?

I hit send, realizing I had maybe not been successful at that delicate balance I was looking for. A moment later, three little dots danced on my screen, and then Owen's words appeared.

> Owen: Dahlia, what's going on?

So perhaps the balance *was* off. I sighed. These were things I wasn't great at.

> Me: We found something down in the
> speakeasy, in the hidden stairwell. Inside
> a barrel.

> Owen: The suspense is killing me…

> Me: Might have killed this guy too.

The three dots danced again and I cringed. What was that? Was I trying to make a joke? Someone was dead. In my basement.

Me: Sorry. That wasn't funny. I don't know why I typed that. There's a lot going on here.

Owen: Is someone dead?

Me: Yes, but no one we know. I don't think. And he's been dead a while. Or maybe it's a she. I don't know.

Owen: DAHLIA

Me: There is a body in a barrel in the bar in the basement.

I typed the last bit as fast as I could, and had barely hit "send" when my phone rang, and Owen's name appeared.

"Hi," I said, feeling a little sheepish about my inability to successfully not intrude on his holiday.

"Why didn't you just call me?" he asked.

"I was trying not to intrude."

"It's fine," Owen said, his voice kind as ever. "And I think finding a body precludes any social niceties you might be trying to preserve."

"Oh, okay. Well, so next time I'll know that."

"I really hope there aren't going to be a lot more bodies in our future, Dahlia."

"There have been a few," I said, thinking back over the odd year I'd been having. It had been a great year, but there had been more bodies than in a typical year, now that

I thought about it. Especially since typical years had no bodies at all.

"Tell me exactly what you found."

I described the situation in the speakeasy, telling him about Zeke and the barrels.

"Are they still down there?"

"Yes," I confirmed.

"And no guests have any reason to be in there, right?"

"Right. It's sealed off. Unless they're looking for the door in the laundry, they won't find it. I suppose there is a chance Margaret knows about the bar, of course."

"I'm glad it's sealed off for now. Hopefully she won't be venturing down there." Owen paused, and I could picture his face as he thought about what to do next, his bright green eyes gleaming, his eyebrows drawn together a bit beneath his sandy hair. "Well, I promised Dad and Elsa I'd take them to tour the mission and see some of the coast and then go to dinner, and they're basically sitting here waiting for me right now. It might be a while before I can get over there. Given the clear age of the case, I feel like it would be okay if I come first thing in the morning. Is that okay with you?"

"Of course," I said. It really hadn't affected me these last few months having a body in the inn, and the only thing that had changed was my awareness of it.

"I'll come now if you're uncomfortable. Or scared."

"I'm not scared, Owen," I said, sensing that he was

trying to be a good boyfriend in offering this. "Tomorrow will be fine."

"I'll call the chief and let him know," he said. "And I'll see you first thing. Eight?"

"That sounds good."

"Okay, Dahlia. Have a good night. I'll see you in the morning."

"Have a good night, Owen." I ended the call and turned to see Diantha staring at me from where she stood in the kitchen doorway.

"You're in lo-o-o-ve," she teased.

"We are good friends," I agreed.

"You're blushing."

"Well..." I didn't have an answer for that.

"What were you talking about? Something in the speakeasy?" Diantha wandered toward me, a smear of red frosting on her cheek.

I wasn't eager to tell her about the body, but I also wasn't used to hiding things from my niece. "I did find something in the speakeasy, yes. I'd like you to stay away from there for now, okay?"

"You already banned me while construction is going on, remember?"

"Well, construction is on hold for the holiday. And maybe longer because of the...thing we found."

Diantha's eyes rounded. "Did you find a body, Aunt Dolly?" She looked abnormally enthused about this.

"I want to say no because you seem overly excited by that idea. But yes. There is a body in a barrel in the bar in the basement and it appears it has been there quite some time."

"A body in a barrel in the bar in the basement," Diantha repeated. Then she giggled.

"Danny, someone is dead."

She stopped giggling. "Right. Who is it?"

"I have no idea."

She nodded, her face taking on a serious expression. "We shouldn't tell the guests."

"Definitely not."

She nodded again. "Also, I'm done with the candy canes."

"Oh good," I said, following her to the kitchen. Diantha had done an excellent job with the cookies, and three dozen of them sat in neat rows on the waxed paper on the countertop.

"Those look perfect," I told her. "Can you put a dozen on a plate and carry them out, please?"

"Sure!"

"Maybe just wipe your face first?"

She frowned at me. "Frosting?"

I nodded, and Diantha disappeared out of the kitchen to clean her face.

Chapter Four

I spent as long as I felt I could tidying the apartment's rooms for a potential unplanned tour by Margaret. As a young girl, I imagined she probably lived in Diantha's room or maybe the room we now had available for houseguests, so I spent most of my time tucking things away in those rooms and making sure they were neat.

When I stepped back out into the lobby, more guests were arriving.

Diantha held Taco's collar, and I noticed Isabelle was at her side and the two were deep in conversation near the fire.

The rest of the group was hugging and exclaiming loudly to one another as they reunited.

Amal greeted the newcomers with a friendly smile, and I moved to her side. When they turned to us after saying their hellos to their family, I spoke. "Hello and welcome to the Saltcliff Bed and Breakfast. We're so honored to host you for the holiday."

"It took forever to get here." This was spoken by a tall, thin woman with a shock of curls atop her head. "I'm Emily, Margaret's daughter. This is my brother Eric, his wife Vanessa, and their children Oliver and Lily."

Amal and I both said hello to each new member of the party.

"The place looks amazing," Vanessa said with a friendly smile. She wore dark plastic-framed glasses and a bright red and green plaid scarf tied around her shoulders. There were glittering drops of water on her shoulders, which Eric brushed away.

"Warm and dry too, which is more than I can say for the outdoors at the moment," Eric laughed.

"You don't really think this rain is going to turn to snow, do you? On the central coast?" Emily looked as skeptical as everyone I'd spoken to in town seemed to feel.

"I very much doubt it," Amal said reassuringly.

"Come in and get comfortable," I suggested, motioning to the sideboard, where the cookies had joined the cake, Madelines, and toddies. "We'll get your rooms sorted and then get to work on dinner."

"It's so kind of you to extend your usual catering to accommodate us," Vanessa said.

"Mom is paying for it," Emily pointed out before offering me a pained smile. I smiled back, not sure what to make of Emily's less-than-cheerful greeting. "No offense, I'm just saying. It's not like it's a charity."

"Still," Eric said, dropping an arm around his wife's shoulders. "I'm sure Ms. Vale had plenty of ways she might like to spend her own holiday week, and here she is, hosting us."

"Oh no, I really didn't," I assured them, earning me a frown from Amal. But I wasn't exaggerating just to make them feel better. I had no family except for Diantha. Where else would I be? Past Christmases had been quiet affairs, just me and Taco Dog in my little apartment in Virginia.

The family moved into the comfortable front room of the inn, taking mugs and little plates of sweets into their laps as they chatted and exchanged the usual greetings and pleasantries. The children, Oliver and Lily, rushed to meet Taco and to say hello to their older cousin, who seemed to have made fast friends with Diantha.

"Eric," Amal said, carrying two sets of keys to the bald man with the short dark scruff on his chin. "This is the key to the Gatsby suite where you and Vanessa will stay. And here is the key to the Atticus suite next door. That one has two double beds for the kids, and a connecting door."

"Perfect," Eric said with a smile. "Thanks so much. We're so excited to stay with you."

I turned to Emily, handing her the key for the Emma

Suite, the only other room on the first floor. "You'll be across from your mother," I told her.

"This is so amazing," Eric said, grinning at the group. "It's so great to get to spend the holidays together like this. Thanks for the great idea, Mom."

"And for footing the bill for the whole thing," Emily said, sounding a bit less grateful than her younger brother. "Though honestly, we could have just come home like we usually do and saved you the cost."

Amal and I exchanged a look. Families were complicated. At least I didn't have any of that to deal with.

"Dinner will be served at six-thirty in the dining room, which is just through that doorway," I told the group, gesturing through the large arched doorway to the dining room just beyond, where a long table could easily seat sixteen people. "And you are welcome to cocktails ahead of dinner. The bar will be set up here at five." I gestured to the bar cart at one side of the room. I made a point of refreshing the ice and alcohol ahead of each afternoon.

Amal and I were attending to a few administrative details behind the desk when I heard Isabelle ask her grandmother if she could see the pocket watch one more time. When Margaret handed it to the girl, she carried it near the desk, to show her mother.

"See?" Isabelle said, holding it out proudly. "And it has an inscription on the back."

"What does it say, honey?" Sabrina had come close and was peering at the watch along with the kids.

"It's so romantic," Isabelle sighed. "It says: Our love endures in every chapter."

"That is romantic," Sabrina agreed. "Whose was it?" She directed this question to Margaret.

"I always assumed it was my grandfather's," Margaret said. "But I suppose I don't have any real reason to think that. It was in his possession when he died, but it could have belonged to my father or maybe someone else in the family, I guess."

Peter stepped close and took the watch from his daughter's hand. "Fine craftsmanship," he said, peering at it. "I don't think it could possibly be old enough to have been your grandfather's," he said, handing it to Emily, who was reaching out her hand to inspect the watch.

"Why, because you're an expert in old jewelry now?" Emily said, her voice carrying a tone that was not altogether friendly.

"I know more about quality jewelry than someone who only shops at the Goodwill," Peter said. "Is that where you got that crazy collection of crap?" He gestured to the multiple silver chains with turquoise stones that Emily wore.

"Peter!" Sabrina said, clearly embarrassed at her husband's open assessment of his sister's style. "I think they're lovely, Emily."

"Sure you do," Emily said, turning the watch over in her hand. "It is really nice, Mom. You could probably get a lot for it if you ever needed to sell it. Gold is really valuable right now."

"I have no plans to sell it," Margaret said, reaching her hand out for the watch. "It's a family heirloom."

Peter clucked and rolled his eyes as his wife whispered something in his ear.

Vanessa dropped into the seat next to Margaret and inspected the watch. "I wish we knew a little more about it. I feel like you can just sense the history oozing out of it. There's a story in that inscription, too."

"I'm sure there is, dear," Margaret said, smiling at her daughter-in-law. "But I'm afraid it's been lost to history, like so much of our family's past."

"I'm going to head back and get the roast started," I told Amal. I had just a few hours to get dinner on the table, and while I was used to baking for dozens of people, I was less used to turning out proper meals for more than three.

"I'll be back in just a moment to lend a hand," she said. Then her eyes slid past me and widened as she looked out the window. "Dahlia..."

I turned to follow her gaze to see the rain coming down in a downpour. The worrying thing, though, was that not all of what was coming down was rain. Some of it was turning to slush as it hit the railing of the back deck, the temperature clearly hovering in a place just above freezing.

"Sleet," I said. "If it gets much colder, that's going to turn to freezing rain, and could cause some real problems." Ice storms had wreaked havoc on the East coast a few times while I'd lived in Virginia. The ice tended to wrap electrical wires, weighing them down and snapping them and could easily do the same thing to tree limbs.

"Well, night is falling," Amal said. "I don't think it's going to get any warmer."

"The guests are all here, no one needs to go out. You can sleep here if you need to," I told her.

Amal looked worried. "I might run home and get a few things just in case..."

"Go before it gets worse then," I suggested, glancing back outside to where drops of precipitation were landing in slushy little piles all over the deck.

"I'll be right back." Amal moved to the front closet, pulled on her coat, and headed outside into the storm.

Chapter Five

Amal returned just as I was peeling the last potato.

"Sorry about that," she said, her voice carrying an element of stress in the breathy way she delivered her apology.

I put down the peeler and gazed at my friend. Her hair was wet around her hairline and clinging to her very rosy cheeks. "It's getting worse out there, isn't it?"

She nodded, giving herself a little squeeze and rubbing her hands up and down her upper arms. "It's freezing. Literally, I guess. My car slid around a bit, but I made it safely home and back. The streets are icing up."

Well, that wasn't good. I hoped Owen had put off the sightseeing until the weather improved. It was a terrible afternoon to drive the coast.

"Are the Donovans all still here?" I asked. "We

should advise them to stay inside as long as this storm is going on. I'd hate to have someone slip and fall on an icy sidewalk."

Amal shook her head. "No one in their right mind would go out for a walk in this," she said. "Plus, on my way in, the older son—Peter, is it?—asked for another pitcher of toddies."

"Oh." That was a lot of whiskey already gone, and it wasn't even cocktail hour officially. But it was the holidays, I supposed. "Sure, if you'll bring in the pitcher, I'll make another batch."

Amal went to get the pitcher, and we made a second batch of toddies for the family.

"Danny seems to have made a friend," Amal noted when she returned and began prepping the carrots and green beans. "She and Isabelle are whispering together as if they've known each other all their lives."

"They do seem to be hitting it off," I agreed. "I'm glad."

"What did Owen say about the..."

"The body in the barrel in the bar in the basement?"

"Yes," she said cautiously, then with a laugh, she repeated. "The body in the barrel in the bar in the basement."

I was laughing now too, and I had to pause in my potato chopping to wipe my eyes. Who knew alliteration could be funny?

"Owen will be over in the morning. He called the chief

to let him know about it, but since it's clearly been there a while I don't think there's much urgency."

"Other than for us to have a bar in the basement that does not feature a body in a barrel," Amal pointed out.

"Right." The speakeasy wasn't supposed to open anytime soon, so it wasn't as if our mysterious guest was delaying anything, exactly. Still, it would be nice to have a corpse-free establishment and to find out who had been in that barrel all those years and why.

"I can't believe they've been here all along," Amal mused as she pulled open the refrigerator. "Is there a glaze for the carrots?"

"Recipe here," I said, handing her a notecard.

"Ah. Good."

"Yes," I agreed, thinking of the body again. "If I believed in ghosts, I might suggest that this could explain Mr. Brown." Whenever there were odd noises or something went missing in the inn, it was attributed to our supposed ghost, Mr. Brown.

Amal smiled at this. "Daisy would love that. You know she believed in Mr. Brown."

"She really did?" I knew my sister had been more drawn to the supernatural than I ever was. I liked things with explanations. Daisy could live with ambiguity and enjoyed the element of uncertainty things like ghosts and UFOs brought with them.

Amal nodded. "She didn't think Mr. Brown was a

problem. She thought he added to the mystique of the inn."

"Well, I hope that isn't him in the barrel," I said.

"If it is, I wonder how he got into a barrel."

"In the bar in the basement," I finished, because I simply couldn't help myself.

As the meal came together, Amal and I talked and laughed, and I had the realization that this was the first holiday I'd had in years that felt in any way special. Having Amal here, and Diantha, and even the Donovans, made the week feel like an event, and there was an unfamiliar warmth inside me. This, I thought, was what the holidays were meant to feel like.

I was about to carry things out to the dining room when my phone vibrated in my pocket with a call.

It was Owen.

"Owen, hi."

"Hey," he said, his voice full of familiarity that made something low in my stomach turn over. "Sorry to bother you again."

"No, I'm glad to hear from you. How's your family? You didn't go for a drive, did you?"

"It started getting icy right after we talked, so we shifted plans to a pizza and a Christmas movie marathon. We're watching *Die Hard* 2 now."

"That is not a Christmas movie."

"Agree to disagree," Owen laughed. "That isn't why I

called, actually. I called because the chief is not excited about leaving you with a body in the basement."

"In a barrel in the bar," I added, unable to stop.

Owen chuckled. "Right. Well, despite the attractive alliteration of the whole situation, he's sending a van over to get it out of there."

"In this weather?" I glanced outside to where the street gleamed beneath the glow of the streetlights, shimmering in an unnatural way that suggested it was beginning to ice over. The rain had not let up at all.

"I guess so. There will probably be a couple guys knocking at the door soon. If you could just show them how to get the van down to the back door and open it for them, they'll do the rest."

"Okay. I guess it will be good to have that out of the inn."

"And we'll be able to get a few questions answered sooner this way. Like how old the body is, and whether it's a man or a woman."

"And if there is any clear sign of a murder."

"Yes. Though if a body is stuffed into a barrel, I think it's pretty safe to say someone put it there, and it's likely that whoever put it there didn't want it to be found."

"Right. True. Good point. So definitely a murder, then."

"Nothing's definite yet," Owen said. "But we'll know more soon. How's the Donovan family?"

"Good, I think. We're about to serve dinner."

"I'll let you get to it. Hopefully, the guys won't interrupt too much."

"I just hope they can get here with all the ice."

"Call me tonight just to confirm it's all handled?" Owen suggested.

"Sure. Talk to you later."

We hung up and I told Amal what was going on.

"Hopefully we can take care of that without the Donovans noticing anything odd," she said.

I agreed, and together, we began carrying dishes out to the dining room.

When the Donovans were all seated, and Amal, Diantha, and I moved to leave them to their meal, Margaret protested.

"Why are there no seats for you?" she asked.

"Mom, I'm sure they have their own plans," Emily said, reaching for the red wine at the center of the table.

"Nonsense. We're in their home, they should be joining us for this lovely meal." Margaret stood and gave me a direct look that suggested there would be no further arguments. "I insist."

There was plenty of room at the enormous table to bring in three more place settings, though I wasn't sure how appropriate it was for us to join the family.

"This is a holiday family meal. For your family," I said.

"You live in my family home and run my family business," Margaret said. "Which makes you my family as much as anything else would. Please join us."

"Yes, please do," Vanessa said.

"Danny, sit by me!" Isabelle called, scooting her place setting to one side.

"If you're sure," I said, addressing the rest of the table.

"Why not?" Peter said, waving a hand from the head of the table as if he would allow this inconvenience just this once.

Soon, three more settings were in place and Amal, Diantha, and I were seated at the table too.

Just as I took my first bite of roast beef, which was surprisingly tender, there was a loud knock at the front door.

"Who could that be?" Margaret wondered aloud.

"I apologize," I said, rising. "Just a minor administrative detail."

"I'll take care of it, Dahlia," Amal said, standing. "Excuse me for one moment."

I sat back down as Amal went to handle the removal of the body.

"This is a lovely meal," Sabrina said. "These carrots are

delicious. I find it hard to believe you don't cater full meals regularly. You're so good at it."

"Thank you," I said.

"Aunt Dolly is usually more of a baker," Diantha supplied. "She can bake anything."

"Wow," Isabelle said, her eyes on me. "Really? Baking is so tedious and exact."

Exactly why I liked it.

"Can you bake a Star Wars cake?" Oliver asked from his spot next to Eric.

"I could certainly try," I said. "I've never made one before."

"You have to make it in a circle." Oliver waved his arms around. "Like the Death Star."

"Oh, well. That adds a challenge," I said.

Peter had turned and was squinting out the windows to the front of the inn, obviously watching the men who'd come to the door return to drive around to the basement.

"Boy, that is nasty weather. Hey, is that a coroner's van?" he asked.

I cringed. "Er... Why would you think that?"

He turned to look at me. "Mostly because it says 'Coroner' pretty clearly along the side."

Everyone at the table turned to look at me.

"Dahlia, is there something you're not telling us?" Margaret asked kindly.

I was not a good liar. And as I considered my next

words, I saw no real reason to lie. It wasn't as if someone was murdered while the family was here today. It was just unfortunate timing.

I explained to the family about the speakeasy we'd found downstairs and our plans to renovate and reopen it in the spring.

"I'd almost forgotten about the club down there," Margaret exclaimed, her eyes misting for a moment with memory. "I used to play down there when I was a child, but my father—"

"Mom, not now." Peter's tone was soft, but it didn't change the fact that he'd just interrupted his mother and effectively told her to "shush." I swallowed down the irritation I felt at his behavior.

"During the renovation, a discovery was made right before you arrived." I finished the explanation, being somewhat careful with my words considering there were children listening.

"So there is a body in a barrel in the bar in the basement?" Eric asked in a steady voice with a hint of amusement in his tone, clearly appreciating alliteration as I did.

Peter was less amused. "You might have mentioned this earlier."

"Why, Peter?" Emily asked. "So you could go investigate? You're an expert on old watches now, I guess. Are you an expert on old bodies, too?"

Peter made a face at his sister, and Vanessa spoke before Peter could say anything else.

"Well, that's rather fascinating, isn't it? If it's been hidden in the speakeasy, do you suppose it's been there since the bar ceased operations?" Vanessa looked to Margaret, who would be the obvious choice for any history of the inn.

"There was a speakeasy, I do know that much," she said, appearing to be trying not to get nostalgic out of possible concern of being quieted again. "My Auntie Evelyn actually told me about it. When she and my father were young, Prohibition was in full force, and their father —my grandfather George—took advantage, if you know what I mean."

"Holy smokes," Eric said. "You never told us that!"

"Your grandmother wasn't fond of discussing it," Margaret said. "Mama said it brought back bad memories and she was glad when it was shut down."

"Shut down, like by the authorities?" Emily asked.

"Well, I don't know really. But I always thought that once Prohibition ended, Grandfather probably just didn't see any reason to keep it open." Margaret took a bite of potato, seemingly done with her story.

Amal stepped back into the dining room and retook her seat. "Apologies," she said.

"Did they take the body?" Isabelle asked.

Amal turned to me with wide eyes. "So I see you've been chatting while I've been away."

I nodded, shrugging my apology. "Yes, they know. If the coroner had come in a more covert vehicle, it wouldn't have been necessary."

"It's really fine," Vanessa said, clearly used to being a peace maker. "None of us are affected at all."

Amal sighed. "Well, it's all handled. They took it and the men told me they'll be getting in touch with Owen as soon as they know anything."

"He's the local detective," I explained.

"And Aunt Dolly's boyfriend," Diantha added with a giggle.

Isabelle giggled too, and I could see that she was of the age where the idea of romance was very intriguing to her. Daisy had been like that once too. I, however, seemed to have missed that stage of childhood. Where Daisy had found boys fascinating and enticing, I found them loud and confusing. My opinions had shifted slightly as an adult, but I was still not wildly talented when it came to navigating social dynamics between the genders.

When dinner ended, I served the pumpkin pie I'd made for dessert, and then set up coffee in the lobby and bid the family goodnight.

I let Taco out into the front garden, but he was reluctant to venture into what had become a completely unfamiliar environment compared to the one he'd seen that morning. Ice coated almost everything, and the temperature was frigid.

He trotted out to the beginning of the pathway and stepped off, doing what needed doing and then shaking his paws unhappily as he made his way back inside. I got a towel and wiped his feet to make sure no ice was caught between his toe pads.

Amal was finishing up at the front desk, and I turned to her. "You really should just stay. It's awful outside."

She nodded, biting her bottom lip. "I figured. I'll take the Holden suite?"

The Holden was the room that had often been reported to be haunted by the inn's resident ghost, Mr. Brown. Recently, we'd discovered that the stairway inside the speakeasy led directly up to the bathroom of the Holden. In the recent past, the speakeasy had been accessible via a network of tunnels around Saltcliff, and there'd been a few local kids making use of them. They'd had access to the underground bar through long-forgotten tunnels that had since been shut down. When that was discovered, I felt confident we'd found the source of the noise and that was usually attributed to "the ghost."

We usually didn't put guests in the room unless we were completely booked. First because of the "ghost," and then because of the stairwell and the potential liability involved if they were to somehow discover it and fall.

"That's a good idea," I said. "You're also welcome to stay with us in the guest room," I said.

"That's okay," she smiled. "Thank you, though. I'll have my own bathroom if I take the suite upstairs, and can keep an eye on the guests better from there."

"That's true. Okay." I'd sleep better knowing Amal wasn't driving home, though she didn't live far from the inn.

"Good night, everyone," I said, opening the apartment door for Taco to walk through. "Danny, you ready?"

Diantha was scrunched into an armchair next to Isabelle, and they had one of the books from the library spread open on their laps.

"Aunt Dolly, look. Mrs. Donovan found this photo album from when she was young!" Diantha grinned up at me.

"Let's look at it tomorrow, okay?" I suggested.

She sighed, but she nodded, sliding out of the chair and wishing her new friend goodnight.

We headed inside the apartment, locked the door, and said goodnight to one another. Taco went with Diantha. He seemed to make a choice each night about whose room he would sleep in, and sometimes I wondered at the complex dog logic he used to choose. Tonight, he must have sensed that Diantha needed him. Or maybe he just preferred her room sometimes.

I missed always knowing he was right there, at the foot

of my bed. But what I'd lost in nightly companionship, I'd gained back threefold in the form of human family and friends. It seemed like a fair exchange.

Before I headed to bed, I called Owen to let him know that the men had come and gone, and also to tell him that I'd accidentally told the Donovans about the body. He didn't pick up, so I left him a message, once again questioning what information was best shared through which channels of communication. Was voicemail appropriate for news of corpse retrieval?

I followed up with a text, just in case.

Me: Body gone. All is well.

Chapter Six

The next morning I awoke to an odd quality in the very air inside my bedroom. I couldn't quite put my finger on it—something about the way the early morning light filled the room as if reflected off a lake or... I made my way to the big window at the back of my room that looked out to the inn's back yard, and to the Pacific Ocean beyond.

The world was coated in white.

The storm that had rolled in as an ice storm the previous night had shifted somewhere in the cold dark hours and transformed the village of Saltcliff into something from a storybook. Snow continued to fall heavily as I gazed out at the odd juxtaposition between the deep indigo ocean and the stark, white landscape in my near field of view.

It was beautiful... but with all the ice coating the

ground beneath it, this particular snow was also deceptive. And given the rate at which it was still falling, I didn't think we'd seen the worst of it yet.

I was in a bit of a rush, since most mornings saw me up before the sun to bake and tidy the lobby. I'd planned ahead, luckily, but still needed to go clean up the coffee service from the night before and refresh the tea packets and brew fresh coffee.

Taco heard me moving around in the kitchen and came out to greet me as I was putting the egg casserole into one oven and the scones I'd made yesterday into the other.

"Need to go out, buddy?" I asked him, giving his furry face a good rub and kneeling down to pet the shiny brown fur along his back.

I snapped on his collar—Taco never wandered far, but just in case—and let him out the back door. My allergen-sniffing service dog was no stranger to snow, but he seemed to understand that our move to California came with the unspoken promise that freezing paws were a thing of the past, and the face he made as he took his first step was comical.

"I know," I told him, laughing. "But you can just run out and come right back. Be quick!"

He did not look pleased, picking his way gingerly through the snow. I sucked in a breath as his leg slipped sideways with one step, confirming my belief that there was a thick sheet of ice beneath the snow. Very dangerous. I'd need to warn the guests.

Taco returned looking doleful as if he realized this might mean he'd been confined indoors most of the day. I cleaned off his feet and gave him breakfast, and then went out to start the coffee and gather any mugs left from the night before. To my surprise, Isabelle was already snuggled up in an armchair, the album from the night before on her lap. The lobby fireplace was the only wood-burning fire we had in the inn, and it had long since petered out.

"Good morning!" I said. "Let me get this going for you!" I added some kindling to the faintly glowing coals, and slowly added fuel until the fire was merrily roaring again.

"Thanks," she said. "Did you see all the snow?"

"I did," I told her. "And I wanted to be sure to warn you. There's a layer of ice beneath it, so it's very slippery and could be really dangerous to walk on."

"Oh, so no snowmen?"

"Maybe in the front garden if you're careful," I said. "But I'd stay off sidewalks and streets."

She nodded. "Dad will be bummed that we can't go look around town."

I understood that. I felt a little cooped up already myself. I had hoped to walk Taco at some point today and say hello to the friends I seemed to run into almost daily since moving to Saltcliff on the Sea.

"Well, breakfast should be out soon," I told her, just as Amal appeared from the stairway looking bright and fresh in a purple sweater dress that set off her dark skin in a way that made it practically glow. I considered my own jeans and flannel shirt, and wondered if my niece wasn't right about my wardrobe needing a more permanent upgrade. Not today though—I was too busy!

"Good morning," I said to my friend. "Did you sleep well?"

"I did," she said. "All was quiet."

I knew she was referring to our ghost. "Well, that's good."

I went back into the apartment to finish making breakfast, and soon the lobby was full of delicious smells and guests helping themselves to food.

When everyone was settled and eating, I relaxed a little, picking up a bit of the casserole for myself.

"Ladies," Margaret called, angling her head toward Amal and me. "I wondered... did either of you pick up the pocket watch last night as you tidied up? I believe I must have left it on the coffee table here in front of the fire."

"Mom," Peter said, his tone admonishing. "How could you forget something so valuable?"

"You have no idea if it's valuable," Emily snipped.

"I don't know that I left it," Margaret said, ignoring their argumentative tones. "I just think I must have. I looked for it this morning and couldn't find it."

"Oh no!" Vanessa said, looking distraught. "Kids, let's look!" Oliver and Lily immediately dropped to their hands and knees and began crawling around the lobby, peering under furniture. Taco followed Lily, nosing her along as if to help.

"Where did you see it last?" Sabrina asked her mother-in-law.

Eric had begun flipping cushions on the couch and kneeling to the floor to peer beneath it.

"I haven't seen it," I said.

"Me either," Amal added. "But we'll definitely help you find it."

"If you left it out, the dog might have gotten it," Peter said, casting a disapproving look at Taco, who was oblivious to his swipe.

"I doubt that very much," I said, doing my best to maintain a pleasant tone of voice, though Peter was quickly dropping down my list of favorite people in the Donovan family.

We spent the next fifteen minutes or so turning the lobby inside out in a search for the watch, but nothing was found.

"I'm so sorry," I said quietly to the worried matriarch. "Would you like me to come help search your room?"

Margaret patted my hand. "I'm sure it will turn up," she said. "What I really want is for you to come take a look at the old album we found in the library shelves. But first"

—Margaret bent her head and whispered—"any news about the body?"

"Not yet. With the storm and the holiday, it might be a while, but I'll get in touch with Detective Sanderson again soon to find out."

"That's good," she said, making a clucking noise with her mouth.

Together, we went to the couch and sat side by side as Margaret began turning the pages of the album. I'd never noticed it in the shelves, and it was a wonder to see the inn in the pictures after it was first built in 1920. The building itself looked very much as it did now, but the space around it was less developed, none of the cottages and sidewalks that made up the current environment were in the photos. It appeared that the town had grown up around the hotel in some ways.

"This is my father," Margaret said, pointing to a man standing in front of a desk inside a room that I suspected was the lobby we were in now.

"Grandmother, who is this?" Isabelle pointed to another photo as Margaret turned the page. This one showed a young woman and teenaged boy at her side. There was a cursive caption at the bottom of the photo, but it was difficult to read.

"That," Margaret said fondly, "is your grandfather and his sister. My daddy and my Auntie Evelyn." Her finger lingered at the corner of the photograph for a moment.

We continued turning pages, commenting on the changes that had been made to the inn, and trying to imagine a time when ladies wore such elaborate outfits each and every day. Margaret's grandmother Eleanor and her aunt Evelyn appeared to be very glamorous, but perhaps they were simply examples of what women looked like at that time. My flannel shirt felt even more casual than it had when I'd spied Amal's fashionable dress this morning and I made a quick mental note to change when I had a chance.

"Who's this?" Isabelle asked, pointing to a man who'd appeared in a few of the photos. "Does it say Frank Burns? Or maybe Braun?"

Margaret nodded. "I think he worked here, maybe. I never met him, but the name is vaguely familiar. Though maybe only because I've seen it here in this album. There were employees and staff here, of course." Margaret laughed and turned the page. We finished looking through the old album and I excused myself to change and to call Owen.

As I stood before the clothes hanging in the closet—most of them Daisy's things—I let out a sigh. I had never been the fashionable sister between the two of us, and it felt somewhat false to put on a dress just because it seemed like everyone was more put together than I was. I had baking and cooking to do, after all. What I'd put on this morning was perfect for that task. What would be the point of ruining one of Daisy's beautiful dresses with flour and eggs?

I turned away from the closet and pulled up Owen's contact in my phone, sitting heavily on the edge of the bed.

"Dahlia, hi," he said, and I could picture the smile he wore. Thinking of it made me feel better. Owen seemed to like me just as I was. And he'd seen me in plenty of flannel.

"Hi. How was your night?"

"Cold," he laughed. "My house wasn't made for snowy weather. Also, I wanted to suggest you all stay in today if you can. The streets are really icy."

"I figured as much. I've warned the guests."

"That's good, but I'm more concerned about you," he said. "You don't need to go anywhere, right?"

"No," I said. "My responsibilities will keep me strapped to the oven for the next few days." He chuckled as I rushed to add, "I don't mean that literally."

"I know," he said. "It's a fun image either way."

"Have you heard anything from the team that came to pick up the—"

"Are you going to do the alliteration thing again?"

"Is it too much now?"

"Last time, okay?"

"The body in the barrel in the bar in the basement."

Owen laughed. "All they know so far is that it's a man, and he's definitely been there a while."

"How long is a while?"

"They're working on that, but they mentioned that what remains of his clothing suggests the twenties or thirties."

"Wow. And did they say anything about injuries or wounds?"

"Nothing they wanted to commit to yet, but his head is not fully intact."

"Oh. Ouch. Okay."

"Yeah. It's definitely a mystery," Owen said. "I'll let you know if I hear anything else, but things are a bit slow between the weather and the holiday. In the meantime, if you can dig up anything more about the inn's history during that time frame, it might help us learn who the guy is."

"You're in luck." I'd told Owen about the Donovan family being here, but I wasn't sure I'd been clear about their connection to the inn.

"Well, that is lucky," Owen said. "See what you can find out."

"Hopefully Mrs. Donovan will still be willing to chat about history if we can't recover her antique pocket watch. It went missing sometime between last night and this morning."

"That's strange. It's only her family there, right?"

"Yep. Her three children and their families."

"Then I'm sure it was just mislaid somewhere. It'll turn up."

"You're right, I'm sure, though one of her sons is determined to blame Taco for taking it."

"What use would your dog have for a watch?"

"Exactly. Plus, he's been trained to ignore things that he shouldn't touch."

"He's a good boy," Owen said, and his words—along with the sweet way he said them—made me feel better about Peter having accused Taco.

"Well, I'll see what else I can find out about the speakeasy," I said. "I don't know how much Margaret would know about its operation, though. It wasn't running when she was alive, but her father was definitely involved in his younger years."

"Good plan. It's worth asking her. We'll do our best to figure out who the guy in the barrel was and why he ended up there."

"All right," I said, feeling a little sad for the poor man who'd been hidden away for so long in the dark. Had his family looked for him? Missed him? Hadn't they wondered what had happened to him?

"Well," Owen said, "Elsa is insisting that we're going to be baking today."

"Baking, huh?" I grinned. That was usually my department.

"Yep. A cake for after dinner tonight."

"Oooh, what kind of cake?"

"Well, this one is pretty fancy," he said, and I began

imagining complicated cakes with multiple layers and thick buttercream frosting. "It comes in a box."

I laughed. "Betty Crocker's finest?"

"I'm beginner level, Dahlia. I think this is maybe the second cake I've made in my lifetime."

"Well, good luck!"

"Thanks. Hopefully, I'll see you tomorrow at the Christmas Eve party, Dahlia, but I'd plan on cancelling if the weather doesn't clear up soon."

Before the weather forecast had become so dire, we'd planned on hosting friends and neighbors at a party the Donovans had asked to have here at the inn. I wasn't sure if that was still going to happen, given the ice and snow coating the streets outside. "I hope so too," I said.

We hung up, and I thought about the man who'd been in the barrel. How had he gotten there? Who was he? I thought back to the pictures Margaret had shown us this morning. She was my best bet for figuring out why the barrels had been hidden in the inn's speakeasy in the first place. I hoped she'd have some information that could help.

Chapter Seven

I ventured back out to the lobby, where Amal was standing behind the reception desk, sorting through some mail we'd let stack up.

Diantha had joined Isabelle on the couch, and they were talking in whispers and laughing together. I was happy to see my niece with a friend. It would make being essentially snowed in a bit less difficult, I hoped. For her, at least.

"We'll have to come up with some kind of lunch today," I whispered to Amal. "The streets aren't clear, and I don't want the Donovans out wandering around. I think it's safe to say none of them came prepared with snow gear."

"I'm sure you're right." Amal put a long finger to her lip. "Can we just do sandwiches?"

I nodded. "That should be possible. There's some roast

left from last night's dinner, and I think I have enough deli meat to put together a kind of buffet."

"That's a good idea," Amal said. "They can make it themselves. Just put out bread and lettuce and condiments."

Margaret was still sitting in the armchair near the fire, while Diantha and Isabelle headed up the stairs, assumedly to Isabelle's room.

"Mrs. Donovan," I said. "Has the watch turned up?"

The older woman gazed up at me with sad eyes. "Unfortunately, no, but I'm sure it will. Watches don't just walk away." She shook her head. "I guess it's possible I just misplaced it. Peter is always telling me I'm starting to lose my marbles." Her face was so sad as she said this, I rushed to reassure her.

"It doesn't seem that way at all to me. In fact, I was hoping we could talk some more about the inn's history soon. You're a wealth of historical information."

Margaret smiled up at me. "Thank you, Dahlia. I'd love to tell you whatever I manage to remember. I'm sure that watch will reappear. It has to be here somewhere."

"True. Well, we'll do whatever we can to help find it." I wrung my hands, unsure how to tell her that I needed the family to stay inside all day today. I had no authority to put the Donovans on house arrest, but I certainly didn't want any of them getting injured on the icy streets. "I also wanted to suggest that everyone remain inside until the storm has passed and the streets and sidewalks have been cleared," I said.

"What?" Peter overheard this and moved close. "We have plans for lunch and we're going to do some shopping today in town."

I doubted very much that anything in town was open. "I'd be happy to call ahead and see if the places you'd hoped to visit will be open. We're just not used to this kind of weather here in Saltcliff, and the ice under the snow is making travel very dangerous right now."

"Well, good thing we're not traveling, just walking." Peter delivered this in a self-satisfied tone that I did not enjoy.

"She's saying the sidewalks are frozen," Eric clarified for his brother. "Did you bring snow boots?"

Peter rolled his eyes. "It'll be fine, Eric. This isn't the arctic. It's California. And we're not going far, just over to the little antique shop after we hit the Captain's Table."

Sabrina stepped close to her husband's side. "Honey, maybe we should listen to Dahlia—"

"It's literally just water. It's just colder than usual. We'll be fine!" Peter practically shouted this at his wife, and then headed up the stairs, assumedly to prepare to go out.

"We'll be very careful," Sabrina said to me, glancing apologetically at her mother-in-law.

"Why is he always like that?" Eric asked, though he didn't seem to be looking for an answer.

"Some things never change," Emily said, settling on the chair opposite her mother and extracting a beige knitting project from a bag. "He's spoiled and thinks the world revolves around him. Oldest child syndrome."

"So I'm an attention hungry brat and you're the sullen middle child?" Eric asked, laughing.

"If the shoe fits." Emily shrugged. I wondered if Emily ever smiled or enjoyed anything.

The group settled into various corners and couches in the room, and I let Amal know I was going to finish tidying up the apartment so Margaret could come inside and tour it if she still wanted to.

Vanessa and Sabrina had taken seats near where we stood behind the desk, and I overheard a few words.

"He's suddenly so worried about money," Sabrina was saying in a confiding tone. "It's so strange. He used to act like we were literally pulling it off trees in the backyard, and now he's pawning things and worrying about every cent I spend. He's making me buy generic toilet paper."

"The thin kind? Not single ply." Vanessa asked in a mock-horrified tone.

"I mean... it's not that bad."

"I'm kidding. I always buy the generic stuff," Vanessa said. "But Eric and I never had a money tree. We're both teachers," she laughed.

"Right." Sabrina sounded like she regretted mentioning money to Vanessa. "I mean, it's not like we're that well off really. It's just strange how he's changed."

"Do you think there's a reason?"

"I guess there must be. I just don't know what it is."

"Do you really think you'll go out shopping in this snow?" Vanessa asked.

"I hope not, but Peter is determined to go get something appraised at the antique store."

"What is it?"

"He wasn't specific, something he found. Some old piece of jewelry or something."

Vanessa made a little noise in the back of her throat. "Not a watch?"

"Of course not," Sabrina said, a hint of indignation creeping into her voice.

"Just curious," Vanessa said, her tone light.

Amal and I exchanged a glance. Maybe keeping the entire family inside for days would not be as merry a holiday as we'd hoped.

"I know you're not suggesting Peter took that watch," Sabrina said.

"No, no, of course not!"

"I mean, if anyone in this family were going to steal and then pawn a valuable heirloom, it wouldn't be us."

There was a pause, then Vanessa said, "and what does that mean, exactly?"

"Just... you know, that whole money thing. You guys are always struggling and Emily is practically a hobo."

"Excuse me?" Emily said, putting down the knitting project and looking at her sister-in-law.

"Right." Vanessa's voice was tight as she stood up. "Kids, let's get our coats on and check out the snow in the front garden." She turned to me. "That's okay, isn't it? If I let them play a bit?"

The kids were already jumping up and down and heading for the stairs to get their coats.

"Of course," I said. "I wish I had snow gear to lend you, but this is just really abnormal. Do be careful on the ice, though."

"No worries. We won't stay out long. Just feel like we need some fresh air." Vanessa said this while shooting a dark gaze at her sister-in-law. A moment later, she and the children had stepped out the front door, letting a gust of frigid, snow-filled air in behind them.

"They're going to freeze to death," Sabrina said, moving to sit on the couch between Margaret and Emily's chairs.

"Maybe you should go out with them," Emily suggested in a pleasant voice that did not conceal the less-than-pleasant implication of her suggestion.

I slipped into the apartment to put lunch together and finish cleaning up. When I brought the platters of meat and cheese out to lay on the buffet, Diantha and Isabelle came to see what was on offer.

"Oh," Isabelle said, casting me a sorrowful glance.

"You don't like lunchmeat?"

She smiled and said, "Oh no, I do. It's fine. I'd just hoped for some peanut butter. I don't even know why, I haven't had it in forever."

Diantha shook her head. "I'm sure we don't have any. Aunt Dolly is super allergic. That's why we have Taco Dog. He sniffs out legumes for her and peanuts are a legume."

"Oh," Isabelle shot an admiring gaze at Taco, who was lying on his back in his dog bed, all four legs splayed in a manner that didn't portray him in the most professional light. "That's amazing."

"You know," I said, remembering what I'd found in Daisy's cabinets upon moving in. "I think there might be some in the apartment, actually," I told the girl, who rewarded me with a grin.

"I don't want to be any trouble," she added.

"It's no problem. Diantha, can you come get it? And Margaret," I said, addressing the family's matriarch. "I wondered if you'd like to see the apartment again before you have lunch?"

"Oh, yes, I really would love that," she said, rising and following Diantha and me through the big door.

"Be right back, Izzy!" Diantha called behind her.

"So lovely that you girls have made friends," Margaret said, smiling at Diantha.

Once the peanut butter was dispatched to the lobby, I did my best to give Margaret a tour. It was odd, because in some ways it was like I imagined it would be if I gave my sister a tour. How did you show someone their own home?

"This was my bedroom," Margaret said, peering inside Diantha's room. "It used to be papered with a lilac wallpaper, green vines all over it. I had a doll's crib there, and a little white desk right here." The older woman's eyes glassed a bit as she looked around, and I knew she was seeing her own things in place of my niece's.

She explained that the bedroom I used now had been used by her parents, and that her Auntie Evelyn had lived in the guest room, which had been her room in childhood too, but that she'd come to live with Margaret's family when she was older.

"Daddy had my room when he was a boy," she told me. "But, of course when we lived here, he was in the master with my mother."

We walked into the dining room and passed through the doorway to the kitchen.

"Oh, and the basement door is still here. How my grandmother hated this thing," Margaret said, giving me a smile. Then she looked around at the modern kitchen, stainless steel range and ovens shining next to butcher block counters. "Well, this is just amazing. So updated."

She walked around the space, shaking her head. "Glorious, really."

"Margaret," I said. "Why did your grandmother hate the basement door?" I wasn't fond of its location in the kitchen, either, but now that the tunnels were sealed, I no longer got illogical creepy feelings when I was downstairs to store or look for something.

Margaret sighed, but her face lit up. "More history, Dahlia. I wonder if you know that the speakeasy below the hotel and the basement beneath the apartment are connected."

I wanted to tell her that I did know that, but I also wanted to hear anything she might be willing to tell me about what she knew.

"So interesting," I said.

"Well, my grandmother just despised the club. Or more, I think, she hated that her husband was involved in illicit activities at all. She was a teetotaler and the Donovans were a distinguished family, you know. But that was where the money was being made at that time, as I'm sure you're aware."

"I have read about Prohibition, yes."

"Well, George's Gin Joint was popular here in Saltcliff back in the day. A kind of high-end club, I guess. And when the place was running, in the twenties, mostly, my father did some work for his father, carrying out duties for the club."

I glanced at the door again.

"The door," Margaret laughed. "Well, I don't want to go to the basement and check if it's still there—my old knees wouldn't allow it, I don't think—but that basement used to connect to the one beneath the inn via a secret tunnel, and that's how my grandfather would come and go when he was doing things Grandmother didn't approve of. Daddy told me that when I was a little girl."

"That makes sense," I said. "Do you know much else about the club? Did other people work there?"

"Well my father, of course, which my grandmother hated. But my grandfather had a few staff, I think. There was a bartender I remember hearing about, and another man, a bookkeeper, I think. We saw a photo of one of them in the album, remember? I think my Auntie Evelyn was rather sweet on a young man who worked here."

"I see. What happened to them, do you think? The bartender and the bookkeeper?"

Margaret shook her head. "I have no idea. Moved away, went on to get other jobs as people do, I suspect."

I nodded. Of course. That made sense.

"Although," she said slowly, raising a finger to her cheek. "There was some bad business at one point. I hadn't thought of this in years, but Daddy talked about it one time."

"Bad business?" I asked.

Margaret nodded. "There was a mob here in Saltcliff—

an organization that was enmeshed in everything. The politics, the businesses."

I wondered if she could be talking about the Mariners, who'd I'd only recently learned about. "Really?"

She lowered her hand and met my eyes. "I don't know all the details, but from what Daddy said, there were even...murders."

I felt my eyebrows shoot up. Was the body in the barrel a mob hit? "Wow," I said.

"Yes. As I said, very bad business. So you can see why my grandmother didn't want her son involved."

"Definitely."

"I'm sure the employees just moved on, as people do. When Auntie Evelyn lived with us here, she used to talk about a man named Frank, though. About how he was coming back for her someday." Margaret gave me a sad smile. "Of course, Evelyn was a bit senile at the end. Very sad."

"Oh, that is sad." There was a lot to unpack here.

"Well, thank you for the tour. It was wonderful to see the house again," Margaret said. "I think I'm ready for lunch, and then maybe, a nap!"

I showed her to the door and walked her back into the lobby, where the tension seemed to have grown even thicker.

Chapter Eight

Oliver was sniffling on the couch, his mother Vanessa at his side, crooning soft words into his ear. Lily was crouched by the fire, practically touching the glass doors.

Eric was next to his wife, looking concernedly at his son, and Peter and Sabrina were at the dining table, whispering in staccato bursts.

Isabelle and Diantha were at the other end of the dining table, smiling at each other and laughing. They, at least, did not seem tense.

Emily remained in the armchair, knitting furiously.

"Has everyone eaten?" Margaret asked the group. The Christmas tree sparkled merrily in the corner, a stark contrast to the decidedly chilly atmosphere in the room.

"We might need to get some kind of activity going,"

Amal whispered to me. "They're going to tear each other apart before we even get to Christmas Eve."

"What do you mean?" I asked just as Taco appeared at my side, pushing his head into my thigh. He needed to go out.

"Eric openly accused Peter of stealing their mother's watch, and then Peter accused Emily."

"Why would they steal a watch that belongs to someone in their own family?" I asked. It didn't make a lot of sense to me.

"I have no idea, but we'd better find it for them."

"Do you think any of them really took it?" I asked my friend.

She just shook her head and shrugged.

"I can help you, Mom," Emily moved to the side table where Margaret was making herself a sandwich.

"I can make a sandwich." Margaret waved an annoyed hand at her daughter. "Just make your own and eat with me," she said.

Emily followed her mother's directions.

"What happened?" Margaret asked her, peering over her shoulder at the still miserable looking Oliver.

"He slipped on the ice outside and banged his elbow pretty hard, I guess." Emily shook her head. "It isn't like they weren't warned. Dahlia told us it was too dangerous to go wandering around."

Vanessa glared at her sister-in-law and turned back to her son.

"I, for one, think it's lovely to have a winter storm come through when we're at my favorite place in the world," Margaret said.

I moved to where Peter and Sabrina were sitting in silence now. "Have you eaten?" I asked. "I laid out sandwich makings."

"Hardly what we would have gotten at the Captain's Table. You know it won the Central Coast Star?" Peter asked his wife, apparently pretending I wasn't there, or that I didn't have feelings that might be hurt if I were ignored.

"Well, hopefully the weather clears, and you can enjoy a meal there after the holiday," I said, pushing down my desire to rescind the invitation to have a sandwich.

"How long will it take this ice to melt?" Peter asked, his voice grumpy like a little boy's might be. "If we can't go out shopping and look around town, our whole trip is basically ruined."

"Unless you came to spend time with your family," Margaret pointed out from across the room.

"Right," Peter snipped. "And don't forget: a dead body."

"The body was removed yesterday," I reminded him, earning me a quick whack on the arm from Amal.

"That discovery was unfortunate timing," Amal said,

"but there's certainly no reason why it should have any impact on the remainder of your vacation." She smiled at the group gathered in the front rooms of the inn, and I found myself grateful for her calming presence.

I busied myself looking around the lobby once again for the lost pocket watch, wandering down the hallway and poking my head into corners. Unfortunately, the watch didn't seem to have been simply misplaced or kicked into a corner. Someone, I suspected, had taken it. I just wasn't sure why.

The somewhat tense lunch atmosphere dissipated only when most of the family decided to return their rooms for a while to rest after their meals.

"I'm going to head inside and start working on dinner," I told Amal, my mind already reviewing the plans I had for what we'd be serving. Tonight's meal was a beef bourguignon with a butternut squash soup and a winter greens salad with crusty, fresh-baked bread. The bread had been rising since this morning, but I had lots to do on the main course. The bread was also the only part of the meal I felt confident about.

I went back inside and paused before getting to work on dinner. I'd missed a check-in text from Owen, and took a moment to sit and text him back.

Owen: How is everything over there?

Dahlia: Good, except the family doesn't seem to be especially happy to be stuck together. They're in some kind of low-grade conflict most of the time.

Owen: Sounds about right for most families.

Well. I wouldn't really know about that. It had been Daisy and Grandmother and me. And we'd been happy to have each other most of the time. Certainly at Christmas.

Dahlia: They've misplaced a family heirloom, so that's not helping.

Owen: What?

Dahlia: A pocket watch. They're all blaming one another.

Owen: Good times. You okay though?

Dahlia: I'm fine. I got some interesting information this morning, actually. About the history of the inn. Maybe about the man in the barrel.

Owen: Well, I'd love to hear it. Maybe it will make my bad news easier to give you.

Dahlia: Bad news?

Owen: The lab will finish up work today and then shut down until after Christmas except for emergencies. Cold cases don't really mandate work over the holiday.

Dahlia: I guess that makes sense.

Owen: They determined that the cause of death was most likely a blow to the head. The skull is partially crushed.

Dahlia: Well, that's something. Poor guy, though.

Owen: Yeah. So tell me what you learned.

I explained what Margaret had told me when we'd toured the apartment and mentioned what she'd said about the Donovan family's potential connections to organized crime.

Dahlia: Do you think the Mariners put someone in a barrel and hid it?

Owen: Well, it's something to check out, but we have exactly no evidence to prove it.

Dahlia: You don't want to take the vague suggestion of a woman you've never met as evidence?

Owen: Did you just make a joke? Over text, no less?

A blush of pride flashed across my cheeks, warming me despite the chill in the air.

> Dahlia: I think I did.

> Owen: LOL

> Dahlia: I need to go make dinner for the grumpy Donovans.

> Owen: I hope they appreciate all the work you're doing.

> Dahlia: They do, I'm sure.

> Owen: Hope to see you soon. I miss you. Happy Christmas Eve eve.

> Dahlia: That's not an official holiday.

> Owen: It is now.

I put my phone back in my pocket and washed my hands, feeling myself smiling despite the less-than-ideal circumstances surrounding my first Christmas at the inn. Even with the weather, the body, the missing watch, and the disgruntled guests, knowing Owen was thinking of me gave me a little spark of joy I didn't think anything else could impact. What a strange feeling it was.

Chapter Nine

Diantha, Amal, and I had dinner in the apartment, leaving the Donovans to serve themselves from platters on the long dining table, which Amal had decorated with what she referred to as a "tablescape." I'd never heard the term, but what Amal had done was lovely, the white tablecloth laid with a very dark wintry tree branch hung with battery-powered twinkle lights and sparkling red ornaments. There was a silver deer standing on one side, and a silver snowman on the other, and each place was set with red napkins rolled into rings that matched the little statues in the center. There was even a set of holiday China laid out that I hadn't been aware the inn had.

"The table was so beautiful, Amal," Diantha gushed as we sat at the less imposing round table in the kitchen in the apartment. There was a dining room inside the apartment too, but we rarely used it. Maybe for New Year's Eve, I thought.

"I hope they won't get into an all-out fight and destroy it," Amal said.

"I'm sure Margaret will keep things calm," I said.

"Isabelle says they always fight," Diantha said. "She says this is why they never get the family together, but her grandmother insisted this year."

"For any special reason?" Amal asked.

Diantha shrugged. "Izzy thinks she's just tired of her kids hating each other."

I nodded. That made sense.

"I can't imagine having a brother or sister and not loving them," she added wistfully. "How can they be mad when they're all so lucky?"

I glanced at Taco Dog, snuggled in the corner but watching us with alert amber eyes. He was the closest thing Diantha had to a sibling, and with her mother gone, there would never be a chance for a real one.

Amal squeezed my hand softly, her eyes understanding as Daisy's presence seemed to float nearby. There had been a time I'd thought my sibling had just stopped loving me, but I knew better now. Still, it was hard having her gone. I understood Diantha's frustration, and wished I could make the Donovans appreciate one another while they were together.

"Izzy says her dad and mom say terrible things about her aunt and uncle when they're at home."

"About Eric and Emily?" I asked.

"No, about Eric and his wife Vanessa."

"Why?" Amal asked.

"They make fun of them because Eric and Vanessa are so in love."

"They make fun of a happy couple?" Amal sounded horrified.

Diantha shrugged. "Izzy thinks they're jealous. She says Eric and Vanessa have the ultimate love story. She called it a second-chance romance since they dated in high school but then met again after college when they were working at the same school. She said it's a storybook romance with all the tropes."

"Tropes?" I asked. "That's a strange word to use to describe her family."

"Izzy reads a lot of romance books. She says those are the things you look for to know if you'll like a story. The tropes."

"Aha," Amal said with a smile. "Dahlia, this beef is so tender."

"Good." That was a relief. I was a bit worried. The only thing on the table I was one-hundred percent confident about was the bread. And the chocolate cake I'd made for dessert.

"Izzy says the pocket watch proves someone else in her

family had a great love story too." Diantha smiled at this idea.

"It does?" I asked.

"Yeah, the inscription."

I'd almost forgotten about the inscription.

"What did it say again?" Amal asked.

"Our love endures in every chapter," Diantha said, her voice taking on a dreamy quality.

"Well, that does sound romantic," Amal said.

Diantha nodded. "Izzy wants to figure out what it means, so we're looking everywhere."

"Everywhere where?" I asked.

"All around the inn."

"Why would there be clues here?" I asked.

"Because the watch started here. It was Margaret's father's, remember? Or maybe her aunt's?" Diantha's nose scrunched. "We'll figure it out."

"You don't think Isabelle knows where the watch is, do you?" I asked my niece.

She shook her head. "She'd tell me if she knew. She was as upset as everyone else when it was discovered missing. She's been really worried about it."

"I still think it will have to turn up," I said. "There's no one else here, and with the weather, no one has come or gone, and we know none of us took it."

"I promise I didn't," Diantha said earnestly.

"I didn't suspect you at all," I told her.

"Well, I might have taken it," Amal said in a low voice.

Diantha and I both turned to stare at her. "Did you?" Diantha asked.

"Of course not, but I didn't want to be ruled out so easily." Amal grinned. "I can be mysterious. I could have nefarious plans you know nothing about."

"You could," I said, smiling at the idea. "But I doubt you do."

"I don't," Amal said with a sigh. "I'm just boring me."

"You're not boring," Diantha said, leaping to her defense. "Izzy says her aunt Emily is the boring one. All she does is knit and talk about women's rights."

"Well, women's rights are important," Amal said.

"Enough of the Donovans," I said, rising with my plate. "Let's have some cake. After all, we have to celebrate. It's Christmas Eve Eve."

"That is not a thing," Diantha said.

"I think we should make it a thing," I told her.

"Like with traditions that we do every year on this night?" Her eyes sparkled and I exchanged a glance with Amal.

"Definitely. What things should we make into a tradition?" I asked.

Diantha put a finger to her lips. "Chocolate cake for sure," she said slowly. "And maybe a board game? And then we watch a movie?"

"Sounds good to me," Amal said, smiling. "If you don't mind me hanging out."

"You are part of our family," Diantha told her, and I nodded. "You and Taco Dog, Aunt Dolly, and me."

Amal's smile told me how much this touched her, and I was proud of my niece's sweet thoughtfulness.

"Let's clean up and we can eat cake while we play Risk," I said.

"Not Risk," Diantha moaned.

"Monopoly?" I suggested.

"Scrabble?" Amal said hopefully.

"Ticket to Ride," Diantha said, rising and disappearing, only to return with a box holding a game I'd never seen before. She held it up with a grin.

"You'll have to teach us," Amal said.

"It's easy," she assured us. And then she proceeded to win easily while we ate cake and laughed together. We ended our evening on the couches in the living room, watching *Elf*, which Amal assured me was funny. I didn't really understand what made it so funny—it seemed fairly ridiculous to me—but I watched it happily, enjoying the time with my family.

Chapter Ten

I was up early the next morning making cinnamon rolls and a quiche to serve for breakfast. Taco had just been out—though he was reluctant to spend more than a few minutes nosing around the frozen garden —and to my surprise, Diantha joined me in the kitchen before the sun was even fully up.

"Happy Christmas Eve," she said. Her voice was fuzzy with sleep and her hair was adorably mussed in every direction. It had grown since we'd come to live together, and now was almost past her shoulders. My heart beat a funny little pulse inside me when I took a moment to really look at her. She looked like Daisy—like the Daisy I remembered from being young. A deep longing sadness filled me, and I did my best to wipe it away.

"Happy Christmas Eve," I answered. "Why in the world are you up so early? You're on vacation!"

She shrugged, her red flannel PJs nearly touching her ears with the motion. "I thought you might need some help."

Though it felt awkward to me still, I reached for her, bringing my niece in for a hug and holding her there a moment. I wasn't used to much physical contact—it was something I'd avoided most of my life except with those I knew very, very well, and even then, I did not initiate.

My grandmother was sympathetic, always careful to meet my eye before extending a hand for affection. As a child, I didn't understand why I didn't especially want to be touched and snuggled in the way my sister seemed to love, but with time I came to understand myself better. And those who loved me understood me too.

But Diantha, I knew, was more like Daisy. She didn't struggle with emotions and affection, and for her, I wished I didn't. More and more with each passing day, I felt a deep love and responsibility for her inside me. And I wanted her to grow up well-adjusted and openly affectionate in the way I was never able to be. I could use logic to adjust my natural tendency toward avoidance because Diantha deserved my very best efforts. But also... on a purely logical level, I knew I was awfully lucky, having someone to hug.

"Well, if you're really interested in helping, I still need to chop fruit." I released her and pointed to the apples, pears, red grapes, and dragon fruit I'd set out on the counter. "It's all going in that big bowl. Be careful with the knife, though."

"Okay. I'll chop fruit and will be sure not to stab myself," Diantha said. She moved to the sink, pushed up her pajama sleeves and began washing her hands. "Did you ever think about how silly that is, how we tell people to be careful? Like I always hear people say, 'drive safely.' As if whoever they're telling had been planning to drive erratically instead, but now will change their plans since someone who loves them suggested they be careful instead."

"I suppose it goes without saying," I agreed. "But still. It's a very sharp knife."

Diantha rolled her eyes and dried her hands. "I will be very careful with the very sharp knife, Aunt Dolly, I promise." As she picked up the sharp knife, she turned and grinned at me. "Maybe we should have some Christmas music? And hot chocolate?"

I hadn't even thought of that. I smiled at her and washed my own hands, pulling out my phone when they were dry. "Christmas music coming up. And I'll heat some milk for chocolate."

I was rewarded with a happy grin, but there was something in my niece's eyes that didn't look as jubilant as her smile. She didn't say anything else, however, so I let it go as strains of "White Christmas" drifted from the speaker on the windowsill that looked out over the side yard of the inn. The world was still coated in white, though the snow had finally stopped falling. The temperatures were below freezing and were forecast to remain there for the next two days. It looked like it would be a white Christmas, after all.

We finished making breakfast, and I set it out in the lobby while Diantha got dressed. I set the big coffee carafe brewing and filled another with hot chocolate, adjusting the little folded signs in front of each one. It didn't seem that any of the family was awake quite yet, so when Taco Dog joined me but then abruptly swerved toward the front door and began barking, I shooed him back into the apartment.

"What in the world are you barking at, silly?" I asked him.

Taco's big eyes just stared up at me as he sat.

"I hope that's not going to become a regular thing, barking at nothing," I said. "That will make it very tough to do your job, you know."

"What will?" Diantha asked, appearing dressed in red leggings and an oversized green sweater with flashing lights scattered over it. It was, frankly, hideous, but I certainly wouldn't share my thoughts with my niece.

"Barking for no reason. I'm afraid he might have woken the family by barking out in the lobby." Despite my annoyance with my dog, I found myself petting his soft head and rubbing his velvety ears. I was never really angry with him. He was too sweet, and we'd been friends too long. Plus, he'd saved my life twice by alerting when he was supposed to—when the food I was going to eat contained something I was allergic to. How could I ever be truly angry at him after that?

"Why would you bark for no reason?" Diantha asked him, kneeling in front of him and taking his big head in her hands.

Taco responded by sinking to the floor and rolling to his side, exposing his chest for her to rub as he groaned in delight.

"He doesn't seem too worked up about it," I laughed.

"Nah," Diantha said, rubbing vigorously. "He's probably just excited because it's Christmas Eve."

I raised an eyebrow. "I don't think Taco can keep track of the date. Nor do I believe he knows Christmas is special."

"He probably notices us acting differently," Diantha pointed out.

"That's true. He is pretty smart that way."

"Did we get him a gift?"

I had picked up one of his favorite bones, but it was in the freezer. "Oh, yes, but I need to thaw it for the morning. Thank you for the reminder."

Diantha wrinkled her nose. "I hope none of my gifts need to thaw."

"Oh yes, I'll get your side of beef out too."

"Funny."

I went to move Taco's bone to the refrigerator, and as I closed the door, my phone vibrated in my pocket with a call.

Owen.

I suppressed the grin I felt forming on my lips and answered. "Good morning."

"Hope it's not too early to call. I know you're usually up baking."

"It's fine, we've been up a while," I assured him. "Is everything okay?"

"Yep. Merry Christmas Eve."

"Thank you. Merry Christmas Eve to you too. How is your family?"

"They're good. A little stir crazy over here being stuck inside. Hoping it might warm up a bit today so we can start seeing a bit of melt. The plows finally came through, but they just scraped clean a layer of ice. The city guys were out putting salt on the sidewalks, but what we need is the sun!"

"I don't disagree." The plows had made a horrific noise as the blades had pushed the softer snow off the layer of ice below. They'd also dropped what looked like dirt all over the streets, probably to offer traction for vehicles.

"Well, I called because I got a little news as the guys shut down the lab last night, but I didn't want to interrupt your dinner, and then honestly, I forgot about it until the middle of the night."

"Oh? What news?"

"When they cleaned everything out, they found a ring in the barrel with the body. A gold band with an inscription."

"The inscription survived all this time? What did it say?"

"It did. Clear as day. It reads: 'Forever' and then the initials E.D."

"Hmm," my mind raced. "The D could certainly be for Donovan. Though it could also be for a million other things."

"Erectile dysfunction. Emergency dentures. Erotic disco..."

"Really?"

"I'm just saying you're right. E.D. could stand for anything."

"Egregious diction," I tried.

"See? It's almost as fun as alliteration, right?"

"Not quite. I'm thinking the best guess is that the D is for Donovan, though, just given the location and time frame when the ring was probably put in the barrel."

"True. If it is Donovan, I'm sure Mrs. Donovan will want it back," Owen said. "Once we have a positive ID, we can get it returned to her if it's hers."

"Okay. I'll talk to her about it today. Thank you for letting me know."

"Of course." Owen sighed. "I wish I could see you. I

have a gift for you. It doesn't look like there will be a party tonight though with the streets still so icy."

"I have something for you too," I told him, thinking of the package sitting on my dresser. I hoped it would be a good gift. I'd never had a boyfriend before, so I wasn't sure what was appropriate. "I haven't officially cancelled the party, but you're right. It's not looking good."

"Well, hopefully we can exchange gifts tomorrow at some point," he said.

"Okay. Merry Christmas, Owen."

"Merry Christmas, Dahlia."

I hung up, and Taco and I headed back out to the lobby to greet the Donovans, who were seated around the space, enjoying breakfast. I said hello to Amal, who'd spent another night in the Holden suite, and I was about to approach Margaret when Taco Dog started barking incessantly again.

"Taco." I used my command voice, but he simply turned his head to look at me and then went back to barking at the bottom of the plant stand positioned next to the front door. "Taco, stop."

"Your dog is loud," Lily told me, stepping close to my side. Her long blond ponytails fell from either side of her rosy cheeks, making her look like she'd stepped off a holiday card. "And silly."

"He is, and he should not be barking at all. He is trained to bark only when he sniffs an allergen."

Now Oliver was on my other side, the three of us staring at Taco as Peter muttered something in the corner about untrained and misbehaving dogs.

"Maybe he found one," Oliver suggested. "An aller... thing."

I moved to take Taco's collar in hand, bringing him to sit. "Stop," I told him. Then I turned to Oliver, slightly embarrassed that my usually well-behaved dog seemed to have forgotten all his training. "No, allergens are things like peanuts or chickpeas. Things I'm allergic to and can't eat. He barks to protect me."

Lily knelt to inspect the spot Taco was staring at. He tugged against my hold and let out a whine.

"What has gotten into you?" I asked him.

"Nothing a little obedience school can't fix," Peter suggested.

I wanted to respond, but I chose to ignore him. Taco Dog had been through more training than any regular house dog. Obedience school would bore him to tears.

"Does he bark at peanut butter?" Lily asked, turning her little head back to look at me with wide dark eyes.

"He does," I said, a little confused at the timing of the question.

Lily reached behind the leg of the plant stand and pulled something out with her hand. Something that appeared to be coated with peanut butter.

"It's pretty sticky," she said.

Oliver reached out a hand and grabbed the item from his sister, which made her shriek. "Give it back!"

As Oliver's hand opened to reveal the prize, he made a face, wrinkling his nose. "It's covered with goop."

"What is it?" I asked, leaning in as Taco barked again.

"Ooh!" Oliver's voice leaped an octave. "It's that watch! Covered in peanut butter!"

I stared at the item in his hand. It was the watch. And it was, somehow, covered in peanut butter.

Oliver ran to Margaret's side with the sticky object thrust out. "I found your watch, Grammy!"

"I found it," Lily cried, joining her brother.

"Kids," Vanessa said, sounding exasperated.

"Actually, Taco Dog found it," I pointed out, but the family had moved to look at the reclaimed watch and no one was listening.

"Would you like me to get it cleaned up for you?" Amal asked, stepping near.

"Yes please, if you wouldn't mind," Margaret said. Then she glanced at me. "I knew it would turn up. What a smart dog you have."

The smart dog in question had finally relaxed and I released him after giving him verbal rewards and lots of pats for doing his job so reliably. "I'm sorry I didn't listen," I told him.

But the best thing about Taco (and all dogs, I suspected) was that he was very forgiving.

Amal took the watch down to the laundry room to clean the peanut butter off, and I took a seat on the couch at Margaret's side.

"I'm so happy the watch was recovered," I said.

"I am too, dear. I'm just a bit confused about the peanut butter. Do things often go missing here and turn up coated in condiments?"

I considered debating with her about peanut butter's classification as a condiment and thought better of it. "No. This is definitely a first."

"How very odd."

It was. "There is something else I wanted to mention to you."

"Oh?"

"The lab discovered something that had been inside the barrel with the man we found in the basement. There was a ring with an inscription inside it. The inscription read, 'Forever,' and had the initials ED. Does that sound like it might belong to a Donovan?"

Margaret's smile widened and her eyes lit up. "How marvelous. Yes, I suppose it could be. I can only think of Evelyn. I wonder if it was hers. But you say it was found with the man in the barrel?"

"Yes, and we still aren't sure who he is. Or who he was. If the mob really was involved, he could be anyone. The speakeasy might have just been a good place to hide the body."

Margaret nodded. "Evelyn was never in a relationship, so she wouldn't have given anyone a ring with a romantic inscription," she said. "She never married, never dated. She had no one to care for her when she was old, that's why she lived with us."

Isabelle, who had been seated silently in the middle of the couch throughout all the commotion, suddenly spoke. "That's not true, Grammy. Evelyn did date once. She was in love."

We both turned to look at Isabelle, who was staring at her hands twisting in her lap.

"What makes you say that?" I asked.

The girl's eyes shone, and her lip trembled slightly. "Because there is something I haven't told you."

Chapter Eleven

Isabelle waited a moment before speaking again, her pale cheeks coloring beneath her flaxen hair. She took a deep breath, as if gathering her nerve.

"Actually, there are a couple things I should have mentioned earlier, I guess." Isabelle looked much younger than her fifteen years as she said this, and I felt oddly protective of the girl, especially when Diantha slipped onto the couch at her side and they exchanged a look. The rest of Isabelle's family quieted and waited for her to speak.

"So... you remember the inscription on your watch, Grammy? 'Our love endures in every chapter.'"

"Of course, dear."

"Well, it made me wonder. It's just so romantic. And I wanted to know more about who would have gone to the trouble to have that inscribed. And who it would be given to."

"That's natural, honey," Sabrina said. "There's nothing wrong with being curious."

Isabelle glanced at her mother, but the worry in her eyes didn't subside. "Well, after Grammy pulled out that old album, Danny and I started looking for other things in the library bookshelves. I wondered if there wasn't some connection between the watch and the books that have been here for such a long time, since the inscription talks about chapters."

Isabelle paused to take a sip of her hot chocolate, and I saw Diantha give her an encouraging nod as she set it back down.

"We found an old journal. And a stack of letters inside of it."

"Letters from whom? And whose journal?" Emily said, putting down her knitting on her lap.

"Letters to Grammy's Auntie Evelyn. From a man. Frank Brown. And it was Evelyn's journal. That's where the letters were." Isabelle let out a long sigh. "Oh, Grammy, it's so romantic. They were so in love."

Margaret smiled widely and put a hand over her heart as if hearing this satisfied some deep yearning she'd had. "My auntie spoke of him, but no one believed her."

"What was in the journal?" Vanessa asked, having moved to sit on her knees next to the coffee table near the fire.

"I can show you," Isabelle said, smiling. She glanced at Diantha, who jumped in.

"It was all about how much she loved Frank and how they were going to run away together and get married."

"Run away?" Margaret said. "Why would she run away?"

"Maybe Evelyn's father didn't like Frank Brown much," Peter suggested. "Who was this guy anyway?"

"He worked for Grammy's grandfather here at the inn," Isabelle said. "That's what it says in Evelyn's journal. He was the bookkeeper."

"Will you get the journal, darling? And the letters?" Margaret smiled at her oldest granddaughter.

Isabelle nodded and rose, but then sat back down. "I have to tell you one other thing first."

Margaret sat back, waiting.

"I was the one who took the watch."

Emily gasped dramatically, while Sabrina dropped a hand onto her daughter's shoulder. "Honey, why?"

Isabelle shook her head, sending her long blond locks flying. "I didn't mean to keep it or to cause an issue and upset everyone. I just—everyone was passing it around and I didn't really get a chance to get to see it, so I took it from the dresser in your room, Grammy. I was just going to look at it, maybe take a couple pictures of the inscription, and then put it right back so you wouldn't even notice. But you did notice. And soon, everyone was looking for it, and I didn't know what to do."

"Does this explain the peanut butter somehow?" I asked, remembering the girl's request the day before.

Isabelle gave me an apologetic smile. "Danny told me you had really bad allergies and that Taco could sniff out peanuts and stuff. She told me how he found peanuts buried under the floor one time. So I hoped Taco would find the watch if I put peanut butter on it, and then everyone would think it had just gotten lost somehow."

"With peanut butter all over it," Peter said.

"Yeah." Isabelle's smile faltered and her eyes filled with tears. She clearly saw the flaw in her plan.

"No one was hurt, dear. But next time, just ask," Margaret said.

Isabelle stood and leaned down to hug her grand-mother. "I'm so sorry. I didn't mean to upset you, but then I didn't know what to do."

"It's fine. Now please go retrieve the journal and letters. I'm very curious what you've discovered!"

Isabelle disappeared upstairs, and I signaled Diantha to join me for a moment near the reception desk.

"What's up, Aunt Dolly?" she asked.

"I'm assuming you did not know about the watch?" I said. I didn't want to be angry at my niece, but if she had helped to conceal a valuable family heirloom, I wasn't going to be pleased, either.

"I didn't!" Diantha appeared genuinely surprised at the question. "I swear."

"It's all cleaned up," Amal said, coming back into the lobby and showing me the gleaming watch. "None got inside, so that's good."

"Thank you for doing that," I said. "You missed the big reveal." I caught her up on Isabelle's revelations after she'd returned the watch to Margaret.

"Oh, I wonder what's in the journal," Amal said.

"Well, I for one, am not interested in old romance stories. I'm going to read a more important journal, the one from Wall Street," Peter announced, sounding bored with the history of his family that was being unveiled. He excused himself up the stairs, and the atmosphere was surprisingly lighter without his presence. Emily returned to her knitting—I still couldn't tell what it was she was making—and the smaller children had discovered the game cabinet next to the library and were sorting through the games inside.

I remembered Diantha's suggestion from earlier and put on some holiday music and brewed more coffee before drawing a chair close to see what Isabelle and Diantha had learned of Evelyn and Frank's history.

Margaret was turning through pages, smiling. "It starts as her suspecting he might fancy her," she told me, catching my gaze for a moment before reading again. "And then here—on March 23rd, 1922, he asked if she'd like to go for a walk with him."

"But she couldn't," Isabelle quickly adds, pointing to the rest of Evelyn's entry. "Because her family wouldn't approve."

"But why not?" Vanessa asked.

"Evelyn writes that it was because he was her father's employee," Isabelle said. "And not an appropriate companion for her."

"That wasn't unusual in those days," Margaret said. "Families were very involved in the dating and wedding off of their daughters. Especially wealthy families."

Isabelle went on. "So they had to meet in secret. Isn't that so romantic?" She sighed this last part, letting her eyes flutter shut.

"Well, in practical terms," Emily said, leaning forward and dropping her knitting to her lap again, "it was far from romantic. Likely, her family was of a different class than his and therefore, he was seen as a lesser human being just because he was not born to privilege. Add that to the fact that women in the early twenties were only just beginning to assert themselves as actual human beings with minds that worked just as well as men's. She couldn't possibly have been smart enough to know her own heart and mind, right? And there's the whole idea of her not being allowed to go out with any man of her choosing without an escort or chaperone."

Emily's tone made it very clear that she was happy to be past the rules that once governed behavior for her distant relatives.

"But a secret love affair, Aunt Emily! That's romantic, you have to admit," Isabelle was clearly not going to be swayed.

"I do understand why it seems that way," Emily said, picking her knitting back up as Margaret raised the journal once again.

"Evelyn talks about the speakeasy here," Margaret said, turning her head to look at me.

"'*Daddy is keeping Frank very late hours lately and I hardly get to see him at all. It would be one thing if he was in the office at the inn, but he's constantly in the club where I am absolutely not allowed to go. The only times I've seen my darling have been when he's been able to sneak away to meet me in the garden. We have a system set up to exchange messages and arrange meetings. I expect to see him again tonight.*'

"This one is dated 1923, June."

"So this went on quite some time," Eric said. "At least a year."

"You have to read the letters," Isabelle said, pushing one forward to Margaret, who picked it up, clearing her throat.

"'April 23, 1923: My Dearest Evelyn,

I cannot rid my mind of thoughts of you, nor cease counting the hours until we may meet again. The touch of your lips upon mine was the most heavenly sensation I have known, and should the good Lord call me tomorrow, I would go gladly, for I have tasted true happiness in your embrace.

I hope the watch pleases you. To see my small gift resting in your delicate hands fills my heart with joy beyond measure. And this ring? I cannot look at it without feeling my heart swell with admiration and yearning for you.

I am near to setting our plan in motion. Only a little more patience, my darling, and all will be as we wish. If you can, meet me tonight in the garden, where we may steal a moment away from prying eyes.

All my heart belongs to you, and every chapter of my life unfolds for you alone.

Yours ever,

Frank'"

"Isn't that amazing?" Isabelle asked. She and Diantha exchanged longing looks and sighed, sinking back on the couch. I wondered if this time with Isabelle was going to turn my niece into an overly romantic teenager too. "And he says 'every chapter,' just like in the inscription."

"It is romantic," Vanessa said, nodding. "But isn't it sad

too? She was in love with someone she wasn't allowed to be with. What must that be like? To know your parents and the world will disapprove, and to have to sneak around and hide what your heart feels?"

Eric, sitting at his wife's side, put an arm around her shoulders and gave her a gentle squeeze.

"Well, you girls have certainly stumbled on a trove of history here," Margaret said. "I am going to read through the rest of these today and just luxuriate in the knowledge that I have absolutely nothing else I have to do."

I wished I could do the same, especially because there might be information in the letters that could reveal why Frank Brown had ended up in a barrel. The mention of the ring seemed to suggest it was probably him, something the girls didn't seem to be focusing on, for which I was glad. But it was already nearing noon, and I had things to see to.

Originally, we'd planned to have a small holiday party at the inn, with the Donovans as our honored guests and many of our friends around town attending. Now, I wasn't sure if anyone would actually be coming, given the condition of travel in our small town. I needed to make some calls, and then see to the cocktails and dinner preparations, potentially just for the Donovan family.

I let Amal know my plans. "If no one else is coming, I guess the pressure is off a little bit."

"Are you disappointed? The party sounded like a lot of fun. And it wouldn't be a bad thing to infuse a bit of outside energy into this group." She said this last part in a lowered voice, gazing over my shoulder at the remaining Donovans.

"Well, I guess there's still a chance people will come. I'll check in with everyone and see."

"Well, I hope we can still do it. I'm going to head up and freshen up the linens and towels in the guest rooms," she said.

"Amal, will you stay with us through Christmas?" I asked her. She'd already made it clear that she was not traveling or visiting any family for the holidays, but I hoped she'd keep her room upstairs until the streets were clear. Plus, it was nice having her here.

"If that's okay with you," she said. "I'd really like to, actually. I brought clothes for a few days, and there's nothing at home I can't let go for a bit. It's not like anyone is waiting for me there."

I heard what I thought was sadness in her voice, and wished I had a way to take it from her. "Good, then you'll stay," I said, smiling at my friend as we both headed in different directions to see to the business of running our inn.

Chapter Twelve

I spent the afternoon contacting those I'd been expecting to attend the party this evening, surprised that most seemed to be still planning to come. When I spoke to Sylvan about the wisdom of everyone trekking out in the snow and ice, he rebuffed my concerns.

"Dahlia, darling, you leave that to me. I've already been in touch with Valerie and Abbey, Louis and Willow, Tabitha, Chef Tippen, and your boy toy, Owen. I've got it all handled."

"How do you have it handled?" I asked my overconfident friend, doing my best to stifle the blush that arose at the classification of Owen as my "boy toy."

"You don't need to worry about a thing, Dolly girl, but let's just say that my family is very well connected in the realm of ridiculous recreational vehicles that are generally useless." Sylvan laughed merrily at this.

"All right," I said, having very little idea what Sylvan was referring to. "If you're sure everyone will be safe."

"I've put Luigi in charge of safety."

That didn't reassure me at all. Luigi was Sylvan's Bassett Hound. "Okay."

"Festive attire, I expect?"

"Um, sure." I hadn't even considered what I might wear. I'd have to spend some time Googling "festive attire," or maybe Diantha could help.

"See you soon, Doll!" Sylvan had been calling me 'Doll' since our first introduction. I'd become somewhat fond of it, actually.

I went out to the lobby to ensure that the family was still expecting guests this evening and would be ready for a party. Then I cooked, recruiting help from Diantha and even Isabelle. Taco helped by sampling anything that was dropped on the floor.

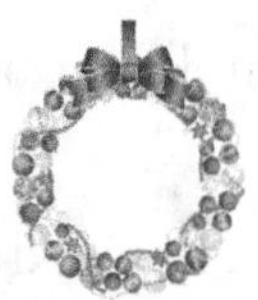

At exactly five o'clock, the sound of some kind of machinery tore through the otherwise silent village outside, and I looked out the front door of the inn to see what might be creating such a racket. To my shock, an enormous tractor-type vehicle was moving slowly up the street on twin treads, making easy work of the slippery surface and loaded with my guests. Sylvan was at the wheel, wearing a bright pink puffy parka, and a red and green plaid hat with earflaps pulled down over his ears. He had a pair of glittering pink goggles strapped to his face too.

"Taxi service has arrived, Doll! Here's your first load of guests. I'll make two more runs to get everyone delivered!" Sylvan waved merrily from the driver's seat as he pulled to a stop and Valerie, Abbey, and Chef Duke Tippen all unloaded, carrying trays and gifts.

"Merry Christmas, honey!" Valerie cried, hobbling carefully up the garden path in high-heeled knee boots that were definitely not made for snow.

"Hello, hello!" called Abbey.

"Hope you're hungry," Chef Tippen said, handing me an enormous, covered platter as he reached the front door. Whatever he'd made smelled amazing, which was no surprise given that the chef was the owner of the Central Star-earning Captain's Table.

"Thank you," I said, unable to suppress my grin at the fact that these friends and neighbors all made such an effort to come, despite the weather. Diantha didn't even bother trying to hide her excitement; she was literally leaping around inside the lobby, dancing and singing to holiday music as Taco scampered around her, trying to figure out what the excitement was about.

Sylvan made two more noisy trips in the snowcat, and

soon, the inn's common rooms were full of guests and the sounds of laughter and chatter layered over the holiday music and crackling fire.

"Dahlia," Owen said, crossing the lobby to pull me into a hug after removing his coat and hanging it in the front closet with everyone else's.

"Hello," I said, feeling oddly shy for no reason I could identify.

"I want you to meet my sister, Elsa, and my father, Gary."

I extended a hand, shaking with Owen's sister—who looked exactly like him with bright green eyes and sandy blond hair—and his father, who could have been a Santa Claus stand-in with his bushy white beard and rotund figure.

"It's so nice to meet you both," I told them. "Thank you for coming. I wasn't sure we'd be having a party after all."

"I'm glad you did, and that Sylvan had access to a snowcat," Owen said. "Who knew?"

I laughed. I definitely hadn't expected that.

"It's a pleasure to meet you, Dahlia," Elsa said, smiling widely. "Owen speaks so highly of you."

"Downright smitten, he is," Gary laughed, smacking Owen on the back.

The Donovans seemed to have blended right into the quirky Saltcliff locals, and I was happy to see Valerie seated next to Margaret with Tessa Damlin on her other side. They all had glasses of punch and little plates of appetizers balanced on their knees.

"When will we play the game, Aunt Dolly?" Diantha appeared before me, still clad in her horrific sweater with the flashing lights and her cheeks rosy with excitement. Amal had told me it was a tribute to ugly Christmas sweaters, but I still didn't see the point of trying to be purposefully unfashionable. I'd changed into a swingy black skirt and a red sweater Diantha had found in Daisy's closet, along with a pair of black tights and low pumps. I felt more festive than I ever had.

"Once everyone has had a chance to eat and drink, I think," I told her. We had organized a game Amal had suggested, where everyone brings a wrapped gift and then has a chance to open a gift or steal one that has already been opened. Diantha had evidently played this game at school before and was very excited about it.

"We can pass out the numbers," Isabelle told me.

"I'll help!" Lily cried, taking the bowl of printed numbers from her cousin.

"Okay," Isabelle said, smiling down at the little girl in the bright red party dress. Her brother Oliver, looking jaunty in his bow tie, was busy inspecting the gifts that had all been piled to one side of the lobby as people had come in. Amal and I had supplied enough for us and the Donovan family, so there was one present to open for every person in attendance.

For an hour or so, everyone circulated, and even Peter appeared to be enjoying himself. The lobby was filled with what I could only call cheer—the sounds of friends laughing, the strains of merry music lingering just beneath the conversation, and the scent of pine, cinnamon, sugar, and rich food. It was warm inside, and though the panes of the windows glimmered with ice and showed that it was becoming very dark beyond the glow of our party, the twinkle lights on the tree and strung from the mantle made me feel light and bright too.

Once everyone had settled a bit, I asked Amal if she would mind announcing the game. The children passed out numbers, and soon, everyone was settled in the main area in chairs, and even on the floor.

"I have number one," Emily announced, rising from the chair where her knitting was—for once—nowhere to be seen. She moved to the large pile of gifts and looked them over. Lily moved to her side. "The small ones are the best," she said eagerly. "Maybe this one, Aunt Em?" She handed her aunt a tiny package I hadn't seen come in.

"My consultant has suggested this one," Emily announced, unwrapping it as she stood in front of everyone. "Oh, this is great. It's a gift card!" Emily held up a gift card to Tidepool Books, Abbey's shop in town.

As she sat back down, Amal called out, "Number two! You can steal Emily's gift card or choose something else."

"What does Aunt Em do if someone steals it?" Lily looked upset at this suggestion.

"She gets to pick another gift," Amal told her with a fond smile.

The game progressed and a pile of wrapping paper and ribbons began to overtake the pile of wrapped gifts over the next hour. There was lots of laughter, a few steals between friends, and in the end, everyone seemed happy with their gifts.

"That was awesome," Diantha said, holding up the snuggly throw blanket she'd unwrapped.

"I'm glad you're having fun," I said, pulling her into my side. My heart felt warm and gooey inside me, and it was easy to identify the fact that being here feeling like part of a family had a lot to do with it. Taco Dog seemed content too, I thought. He'd chased wrapping paper around a bit, and now was curled up on his bed near the door, sleeping.

Owen stepped close and kissed my cheek. "You look beautiful tonight, Dahlia," he said.

I fought the urge to push a hand into my wavy brown hair or adjust my glasses. I had never felt beautiful, but when Owen said it, I almost believed him. "Thank you."

His hand slipped down my arm and his fingers found mine, twining through them. "Do you think we can take a moment away so I can give you your gift?" he asked, a hopeful gleam in his emerald eyes.

I wanted to give him his gift too, and it seemed like

everyone was able to take care of themselves for now. The food was mostly gone, and a few people meandered about, snacking on fudge or cookies. Peter was at the bar cart, happily mixing drinks for those who asked, and the kids were on the ground near the fire with their heads bent together, examining their gifts.

"Sure," I said. "Want to step into the apartment for a minute?"

He nodded. "Let me just let my dad know we'll be right back."

Owen stepped away, and I waited near the door for him to return. When he did, we went into the quiet of the apartment, shutting the big door behind us.

"You outdid yourself. The party was amazing," he said with a smile.

As I looked at him, basking in his praise, I appreciated his open and happy outlook on everything. He was trustworthy and good, and he was patient, which for me, may have been the most important thing.

"Thank you," I told him. "For coming, and for everything else."

"Everything else?"

Emotions rushed through me, and I fought through them. This was the kind of interaction I found very difficult. I knew what I felt, for the most part, but I had a nearly impossible time verbalizing it. "You make me happy," I managed. "You're a good man."

"You make me happy too," Owen said, his easy smile telling me he knew my struggle, and making it clear my words told him what he needed to hear. "Here. Open this." He withdrew a small square package from inside his jacket pocket and handed it to me.

"It's so pretty," I said. The package was wrapped in gold paper and tied with a simple red ribbon.

I led Owen to the couch and sat, the package on my lap, but then I started to get up again. "I have something for you too."

He pulled me back down to sit. "In a minute. Open yours first."

I did, and the simple gold bracelet inside the box very literally stole my breath. "It's beautiful." It felt like a lot—to receive jewelry from a man. "Is it too much though, maybe?"

He laughed. "I had a feeling you might say that. I wanted to get something even bigger with some gleaming stones... but I know you, Dahlia. And I admire you. You're practical and smart, giving and kind. I got you a simple chain because I thought you could probably keep it on even while you're baking, and then maybe sometimes you'll look at it and think of me."

I nodded, unsure what words might fit the situation. I loved the bracelet, but I loved Owen's words even more. I held out my hand and Owen fastened the little chain around my wrist. "I love it," I said.

And then Owen leaned forward a tiny bit, his eyes scanning my face. I knew that if I showed the least little bit of resistance, he wouldn't make a single move, but I wanted to kiss him. So I did. And it was soft and warm and perfect, just like the feelings I had for him.

"Now your gift," I said, jumping to my feet and heading to my bedroom. "Stay there."

I returned with the package and handed it to him, hoping it was a good gift.

Owen opened it and looked down at the contents with his signature wide smile. "Did you make this?" he asked, lifting out the wool scarf I'd crocheted in Qiviut wool.

"I did," I said, smiling. "It's not a lot, but the Qiviut wool comes from the undercoat of the muskox, and it is supposed to be eight times warmer than sheep's wool."

"Is that right?" he asked, his eyes never leaving mine. "I've never heard of it, but I'll take your word for it."

"I special ordered it when it looked like it was going to get really cold."

"I love it," he said, wrapping it around his neck. "Dahlia, it's really amazing. And you made it." This last was spoken with an air of wonder, and it made my heart even gooier and warmer than it had been already. "Thank you."

We hugged for a long moment, and then rose, and Owen took my hand. "I hope to see lots more of each other in the new year. I'm really glad you moved here, Dahlia."

"Me too," I said. "Oh, there's one more thing. About the body in the—"

"Don't ruin the moment with excessive alliteration," Owen laughed.

"Okay, I won't," I agreed. "But I wanted to tell you that Evelyn Donovan, Margaret's aunt, was involved romantically with Frank Brown, the inn's bookkeeper."

"So the E.D. was her?"

"I think so, based on a letter we found from Frank referencing the watch. He also mentioned the ring, so it seems like the body is probably Frank."

Owen's eyes widened a tiny bit.

"Although, I guess it's possible Frank Brown put the body in the barrel and his ring slipped off in the process. Do you think he might have been involved with the Mariners?"

"My research has been a bit stalled given the holiday and my family in town, but at this point, anything is possible."

"Yes, I haven't been digging as much as I'd like, either," I admitted. "But I do know that Evelyn Donovan was involved with a man her family likely didn't approve of. One who had intimate knowledge of her father's business dealings."

Owen was silent a moment as my words sunk in. "We'll figure it out," he said. "Or the guys at the lab will when they're back."

I nodded, knowing he was right. But something in me wanted to get it figured out sooner, and I couldn't help feeling like there was a piece missing.

"Should we head back out?" Owen asked, flipping his scarf around his neck once more.

"Okay," I agreed, and together, we headed back out to the party.

As soon as I stepped through the door, Sylvan flounced near, his pink ruffled neckline flying around his face. "Doll, this shindig has been such a gas," he said, taking my hand in his. "Oh, and look at this!" He admired my new bracelet. "Is this your doing, Officer McHotstuff?"

Owen's cheeks turned pink as he nodded at my friend.

"Well, I hate to do it, but I think the Sylvan Taxi Service needs to begin making its rounds once again to get all these revelers home before Santa pops by for a nightcap. And by Santa, I mean my new beau Santos, who I met at the gym last week." Sylvan gave me a big wink and then burst out laughing, clearly needing no encouragement from anyone else.

"Thank you for bringing everyone," I told him. "You saved Christmas."

"I'm a hero, you know," he agreed. "Maybe I should wear some kind of spandex suit next year. Captain Christmas, you can call me." He giggled and sauntered away as Owen and I exchanged amused looks.

Soon, the lobby was relatively quiet again, with all the

guests departed and the Donovan family beginning to move toward bed.

"There'll be breakfast here in the morning for you," I told Margaret. "But we won't disturb your holiday until the afternoon. That said, just knock or text if you need anything at all," I told her.

"That's kind, but please feel at home," Margaret said. "This is more your home than ours, after all."

"We have our own tree inside, and plenty to keep us occupied," I reminded her. "We'll be fine."

She gave me a long look and pulled me into a hug. "You've made an old woman very happy, Dahlia. Thank you for hosting us. What a wonderful party."

"Wait!" A small voice came from the stairs, and I turned to see Lily and Oliver standing on the bottom step, clad in Christmas pajamas that matched. "What about Santa's cookies? And our stockings?"

The two children held up big red stockings, and Margaret leaned near. "Don't worry, dear, their parents are prepared."

That was good. I hadn't thought to shop for stocking stuffers.

"And I have mine too," Isabelle said, appearing behind them holding a stocking.

"Let's hang them up," I said, taking the stockings. "And maybe you two can go get a plate of cookies for Santa? There are some left on the dining table."

Oliver and Lily rushed to gather a plate of cookies, and I went to the box of decorations behind the front desk, remembering a couple of items I hadn't been sure about when I'd first found them. They were heavy bell-shaped decorations with hooks sticking out from the front. Now I realized they were to hang stockings on the mantel, and the weight ensured they wouldn't topple over.

"Here we go," I said, hanging the big red stockings.

"And this is for Santa," Oliver said, putting the plate next to the fireplace.

Taco stepped close, looking at the plate as drool began to accumulate along his jowls.

"Not for you, buddy," I told him, and the big amber eyes raised to meet mine.

Oliver put an arm around my dog's neck, bending down to look into his face. "You're Taco, not Santa."

"You two, to bed," Margaret said, kissing the littler children and then hugging Isabelle close. "And I'm doing the same. Good night, everyone."

I cleared up some dishes and tidied the last bits of wrapping paper, let Taco out front for a few minutes, and was just about to head inside the apartment when I noticed Diantha and Isabelle pulling books from the shelf, one by one.

"What are you doing?" I asked, trying not to be dismayed at their efforts toward disorganizing what I was busily trying to organize.

"We think we're on to something," Isabelle said.

"What?" I asked, feeling more than ready to lie down.

"Frank and Evelyn had a system for exchanging messages, the journal said so. It's some kind of hiding place only they knew about. We think it was inside a book." Diantha told me this as she continued pulling books out of the shelves.

"Why do you think that?" I asked.

"There have been a ton of literary references in their letters," Isabelle said. "My grandmother noticed them. And the inscription talked about chapters."

"Well, it's something, but I'm not sure that's enough to support your theory. How will you know if you have the right book?"

Isabelle and Diantha exchanged a look.

"Because we think there's a letter still hidden," Isabelle said. "All we have to do is find it."

Chapter Thirteen

I rose once in the wee hours of the morning to attend to Santa's plate of cookies in the lobby. I thought there was a chance that the kids' parents might have thought to take care of it, but I wanted to be sure. We'd put a similar plate up on the mantel inside the apartment too, where Taco couldn't find it in the middle of the night.

The plate in the lobby had been cleared, and I smiled at the overflowing stockings hanging over the dying embers of the fire. I put on a couple more logs, spacing them out to burn slowly, and then went back inside to fill Diantha's stocking.

Almost-teenaged girls were—luckily—fairly easy to shop for if you knew who to ask. Amal had suggested lip balm and lotion, bath bombs and hair accessories. I'd also put in a small electrical programming project I thought would be fun, along with a Rubik's cube. I was all for encouraging Diantha to use makeup and lotions if she wanted to, but I also wanted to encourage her to use her brain.

I broke off a few pieces of the cookies on the plate and took a long swig of the milk, second-guessing that last bit as I swallowed the lukewarm liquid. And then I headed back to bed, satisfied that the morning would unfold as it should, with everyone sure that Santa had made his rounds.

When the first rays of sunlight slanted through the tops of my windows, I stretched and yawned. It was the first Christmas in many years that found me waking up with a sense of excitement glowing in my chest, an eagerness to meet the day and revel in the surprises it might hold. I had a family, I realized with an expanding sense of wonder. And a boyfriend, maybe. And friends, and a whole new life. And it was all thanks to the one person who wasn't here to enjoy it with me.

I spent a long moment in the warmth of my covers, thinking about my sister. Though the memories were old and worn with time, I did my best to pull out a few of the Christmas mornings I remembered from childhood, where Daisy and I hopped out of bed way too early to pick up our stockings and take them back to our bedroom to open together. We'd been allowed to open them before Grandmother was awake, but we had to wait for the rest of the presents until she'd had her second cup of coffee.

Those quiet mornings were joyous—just the two of us, whispering excitedly over the little gifts we found, the thrill of the day to come settling around us like a sparkly blanket.

"I miss you, Daisy," I told her, finally opening my eyes and taking a deep breath.

I dressed in jeans and a warm, soft green sweatshirt, and slipped my feet into a pair of fuzzy slippers. After a quick pass through the bathroom, I headed out to the kitchen to finish breakfast for the guests and get the cinnamon rolls baking for our own Christmas.

Once the coffee was brewed and the food was in the lobby, Amal came through the apartment door, her arms full of gifts. "I had planned to drop these by today, but now we'll just add them to the pile," she said, kneeling to place them under the tree with the others.

"I'm so glad you stayed," Diantha said, moving to wrap her arms around Amal. "You should just spend Christmas here every year."

"You should," I said.

Amal smiled at me, and I thought I saw a flicker of sadness in her dark eyes. Of course, she missed Daisy too.

"I've got coffee, and cinnamon rolls will be ready in a few minutes. Danny, did you already open your stocking?" I asked.

Diantha smiled and nodded. "Please be sure to thank Santa Claus for the lip gloss and the little flashlight kit he left me." She held up a tiny flashlight she'd clearly constructed in the early hours of the morning.

"You already put it together?" I asked. It wasn't a complex kit, but I thought she'd need some help.

"I did," she said, smiling proudly. "Please let Santa know there is a raspberry Pi kit I'd really like next year."

So Diantha was interested in learning coding? "I'll tell him," I said, a glow of pride igniting inside me.

"Raspberry pie?" Amal asked, looking between us.

"A raspberry pi is a single board computer that is used to begin to learn to program and how computers work," I explained.

"Oh!" Amal laughed. "And I thought it just sounded delicious."

"That too," Diantha told her. "When are we doing presents?" She turned away to stare at the tree, which glowed with multicolored lights in the corner of the living room, the gifts all waiting at the bottom.

This was unfamiliar territory for me. What did Daisy do? I looked to Amal and Diantha. "What do you usually do?"

"Mom liked to wait until she'd had two cups of coffee," Diantha said, rolling her eyes and sighing dramatically.

I couldn't help the smile that took over my face. Daisy remembered those early Christmas mornings too. "Then that's what we'll do," I told her. "Lucky for you, I already had one."

Diantha sighed again as we headed for the kitchen to pour another cup of coffee and pull the cinnamon rolls out to cool. Taco Dog had already been out and had his breakfast, but he looked pitifully hopeful when the smell of cinnamon wafted through the kitchen as the rolls were set on the countertop.

"Does Taco have to wait for his gift too?" Diantha asked as I poured Amal a cup of coffee and she took it to the little round table to sit.

"No," I said, "I guess not."

"Where is it?"

I pulled Taco's wrapped bone from the refrigerator—I couldn't put it under the tree, or he would have opened it already. I handed it to Diantha as I took my own coffee to the table to join Amal and placed a cup of hot chocolate at the third place for my niece.

"Come here, Taco," Diantha said, holding the gift high and motioning for Taco to sit.

He did, his eyes on the gift in her hands as his mouth drooled in anticipation of something delicious.

"Here you go, buddy." She put the gift before him, and Taco nosed at it curiously. It wasn't wrapped tightly, and it had no ribbon, but he still looked fairly uncertain.

"I usually have to start it for him," I told her.

Diantha pulled one corner open, and Taco seemed to get the idea from there. We all watched and laughed as he eagerly removed the wrapping paper from the big bone I'd picked up at the Paws Spa gift shop in town. I'd already removed the plastic, so Taco dove straight into enjoying his treat.

"He loves it," Diantha laughed.

"He does," I agreed.

We spent a leisurely morning, eating, drinking, opening gifts, and laughing. Amal gave me a gorgeous cashmere sweater in a deep turquoise color she said would be perfect with my hair, and Diantha gave me a mug she'd made at school and a brooch of a dog that was shaped just like Taco.

They both opened gifts too—Diantha happy to find the Raspberry Pi kit she'd been hoping for, and Amal made appreciative noises about the gift card to the spa I'd selected—and everyone seemed happy with their morning.

When Amal discovered the scarf Diantha had crocheted for her, she put it on immediately with tears lining her cheeks. "I love it."

"Don't cry, Amal." Diantha leaned into her arms and gave her a long hug.

When it was just paper and ribbon left scattered around us, I took a deep breath and stood. "Thank you for this. It was the merriest Christmas I've had in a long time," I told them.

Diantha jumped to her feet and gave me a hug, and then ran to hug Amal. "Mom would be happy to see us together," she said, and I marveled at the maturity it took a twelve-year old girl to find those words. I had thought them, but I hadn't been able to speak them.

Amal nodded. "She would."

"I guess I should see to the guests," I said, heading for the door.

"I'll be right behind you," Amal said. "Danny and I will clean up the paper here."

I headed out to see how the Donovans were doing and make sure they didn't need anything.

The lobby of the inn was scattered with gift wrap and ribbon, and Lily and Oliver were shrieking and leaping around, chasing each other with what appeared to be laser guns.

"They got a laser tag set," Emily said from her spot by the fire. She looked up from her knitting with a sour expression. "Everyone is thrilled with this gift."

The adults all looked a bit overwhelmed, and the sheer amount of noise coming from the guns and the children was enough to encourage me to run back into the apartment. However, I had responsibilities, so I swallowed hard and tried to ignore the chaos.

That was easier said than done when I glanced at the

bookshelves at the far side of the room. Isabelle was seated on the floor, books all around her. Almost every single book had been removed from the shelves. There were piles everywhere, books scattered across the floor where the smaller kids had kicked the piles as they ran around, and the dust that had coated the books seemed to hover in the air. My fingers itched to put it all to rights immediately, but I forced myself to remain calm.

"Isabelle, did you find what you were looking for?"

The girl looked up at me and shook her head. "No, and I've searched every single book now. There's no letter!"

I leaned down and stacked a pile of books back up, unable to help myself. "Why do you believe there is one letter remaining?" I asked.

Isabelle reached into her back pocket and pulled out an aged piece of paper, folded several times. "This."

I opened it and read.

July 16, 1923

    My Beloved Evelyn,

    How I long to hold you again, to speak these words in your ear and to feel the warmth of your hand in mine. But as I must, I set these words to paper, and may they reach you soon.

    Our dreams are nearly within reach, my dearest. I

have prepared what we need and arranged it all. There are a few scant details to wrap up.

These details will be in the last message I will leave for you.

If fate is kind, I will see you at the chosen hour, and together we shall leave behind all that stands between us and a life of our own with the protections we've discussed to assure our security. Should any trouble befall me, may my last word be a token of my love and all that I would have said.

With all that I am,

Frank

I looked up at Isabelle's wide eyes. "How do you know that final message wasn't found yet?"

She shrugged. "I mean... I don't. Not really. But wouldn't it have been here with the rest of the letters if it was? That's the last one, the last date we have."

"July 16," I read. "What do you think he means when he says 'protections' and 'security'?"

"I don't know," Isabelle said, frowning. "But if no one wanted them to be together, maybe they had to do something bad to be sure they could be."

"Something bad?"

"Like maybe they blackmailed someone or something," she said.

I nodded. "Maybe." My eyes trailed over the bookshelves. "Are you sure you've looked everywhere? Maybe it's in the shelf itself somehow?"

She shrugged and stood up, and together, we searched every inch of the shelves. At one point, I tugged a chair over so I could run my hands over the top shelves and feel for any hidden latches or depressions where something might be hidden. All I got for the trouble was very dusty hands.

"She's got you involved now, huh?" Peter strolled across the lobby, a smile on his face that wasn't altogether friendly.

"She's got me curious," I agreed, stepping back down.

"Teenage fantasy and nothing more," he said, waving a dismissive hand at his daughter.

My spine straightened and my mouth opened before I'd decided to speak. "Or," I heard myself say loudly. "An intelligent and curious mind pursuing every possible avenue of exploration in pursuit of the answer to a question no one else has bothered to ask."

A little squeak came from Isabelle at my side, and a glance at her confirmed that she was covering a wide smile.

Peter made a noise that sounded like "humm," and turned away, taking a seat across from Emily, who was smirking at him.

"It's certainly been an enticing mystery," Margaret said, stepping close and glancing down at the books strewn all around. "But maybe we need to take a break and help Dahlia put the inn back together before pursuing it further."

"Oh," Isabelle said, her eyes widening as if she was only now noticing the destruction. "Oh my gosh, of course. I'm sorry."

"Actually," I said, "if you don't mind waiting a moment, I'll just clean the shelves while they're empty. And then you can help me put the books back up."

"Okay," Isabelle said. "Sorry for the mess."

I shook my head. "It's not a problem at all."

Amal had emerged from the apartment and stood nearby, listening.

"Dahlia, I hate to add to the issue, but there are several more boxes of books downstairs. Daisy and I moved them a couple years ago because the books on the shelves were stacked two-deep."

Isabelle and I exchanged a look just as Diantha emerged from the apartment with Taco.

"Danny, there are more books in the basement. Come help me look!" Isabelle ran to Diantha and took her hand.

"Okay!" Diantha said, following her new friend.

I went with them to the laundry room downstairs to get the supplies I'd need to clean the shelves and help them find the boxes.

"Here you go," I said, pulling six heavy boxes off the

shelves. "How about if you put them back in the boxes after you look through each one?"

"Good idea," Isabelle said, her eyes shining with excitement.

I left the girls with the books and went back upstairs, armed with rags and wood cleaning spray.

Chapter Fourteen

Two hours later, the lobby's library was pristine (and alphabetized) and Diantha and Isabelle came sprinting up the stairs from the laundry, both of them talking excitedly at once.

"Great Expectations!" Diantha yelled at the same time as Isabelle cried out, "Pip loved Estella!"

"Girls, girls..." Eric intercepted the two girls at the end of the hallway, calming them as he escorted them into the lobby to sit on the couch by the fire. "Tell us what you're so excited about."

"Did you find something?" Margaret asked, waking from where she'd been dozing by the fire.

"Yes, the last letter," Isabelle said, holding up a folded piece of paper.

"It was in the book 'Great Expectations,'" Diantha said.

"Which is so perfect because Pip was in love with Estella, and they were from different classes, just like Frank and Evelyn!" Isabelle told us.

I was surprised to hear that Isabelle had read Dickens. I was also impressed at the analysis the girls had clearly done.

"There were more journals down there too," Diantha said, her eyes huge. "Like a whole bunch."

"What does the letter say?" Margaret asked.

"It's a little bit confusing," Diantha said, looking at her friend.

Isabelle spread the final letter on her lap, and then in a very serious voice, she read:

"*July 30, 1923*

My Dearest Evelyn,

The time is upon us at last. Tonight, as the hour strikes eleven, I will meet you at the Cypress pine above the cove, where no prying eyes may follow. We shall take only what we need, and nothing shall delay us from the life we have so long planned together.

I have secured the means to keep us safe from those who might seek to do us harm. The ledgers I now possess contain every transaction of the past years, each entry a silent witness to their dealings. These records are our shield, my love, should anyone seek to drag us back to that place we wish so desperately to leave behind. They will ensure we are left to live in peace—this, I promise you.

Trust in me, Evelyn, as I trust in the strength of what we share. With these last arrangements made, I am finally able to do as we have spoken of for so long. Only a few more hours, and then, my beloved, no one shall keep us apart.

Yours, until the end,

Frank"

"What ledgers?" Eric asked.

I knew immediately what ledgers the letter referred to, because I'd discovered them beneath the bar of the speakeasy when I first found the place sealed up behind our laundry room.

"The ledgers record all the transactions in the club," I explained. "But Frank couldn't have taken them because they were still there when I found the speakeasy this fall."

Margaret reached for the letter, reading it once more.

"Why do you suppose Evelyn never got this letter?" she asked. "She must have known where to find it, don't you think? Why was it still in the book?"

I was wondering the exact same thing.

Isabelle shrugged. "It's so sad. They were all ready to go, but she never found the last letter so he must have waited and waited and finally left without her."

Or ended up in a barrel, I thought.

"Did you say there are more journals?" Vanessa asked.

The girls nodded. "A lot of them."

"Maybe the answer is in there?" Vanessa suggested.

"It would take years to go through them," Diantha said.

Vanessa shrugged. "I've got time."

"Me too," Sabrina said. "Let's go."

The women went with the girls back downstairs, leaving the mystery lingering in the lobby.

Amal and I continued cleaning up and then finally went in to prepare dinner for the family for Christmas.

But before I headed into the kitchen to help with the turkey, I wanted to do a bit of digging online.

"I don't mind," Amal told me, pulling the three turkeys we'd brined from the refrigerator. "I can get these started."

Diantha had gone down to look at the journals with the others, so I went into my bedroom and opened my laptop, searching for anything I could find about the Mariners activities in Saltcliff during Prohibition.

Surprisingly, there was quite a lot.

I clicked into an old news item with the headline, "Bootlegger's Haven: Mariners' Smuggling Empire Controls Northern Coast: Local Establishments Under Watch as Mariners Syndicate Extends Its Reach from Port to Parlor." The piece was in the San Francisco Chronicle, dated early 1923. I was just diving into the article when my phone rang.

Owen.

"Hello. Merry Christmas," I said.

"Merry Christmas, Dahlia. Not to discuss morbid topics on a holiday, but I've only just gotten time to do some digging into the Mariners' activities back in the twenties in hopes of figuring out more about our barrel buddy."

"That's what we're calling him now?"

"We don't have to," Owen said with a laugh.

"I'm actually doing the exact same thing," I told him.

"Great minds," he said.

"What have you found?"

"A few things," he told me. Owen described the article I had been about to read and a couple others. "So basically, we know that the bulk of alcohol coming into the central coast during Prohibition was probably controlled by the Mariners. I'd guess that would include whatever supplies were being sold from the speakeasy at the inn."

"George's Gin Joint," I told him. "Margaret told me the name."

"Well, I doubt it was hanging on a sign outside or anything."

"Probably not," I agreed. The door to the bar entered the alley behind the inn, and it looked like a loading area if anything. There was nothing that made it look remotely appealing to anyone who didn't know what they were looking for.

"Do you still have the ledgers you found a while back?" Owen asked.

"We were just talking about them this morning, actually," I told him. I filled Owen in on the last letter and the journals the girls had found.

"If Frank was the bookkeeper, then he certainly knew about the ledgers. He probably recorded all the shipments and sales himself," Owen said. "But why would he be taking them if he was going to run away?"

"The letter said something about every entry being a record of 'their dealings,'" I said. "And it said the ledger would protect them. Do you think he was threatening to go to the authorities?"

"That would put him in hot water with the Donovans and with the Mariners," Owen said. "The question, I guess, is which of them actually killed him?"

I thought about sweet Margaret Donovan. Could someone in her family tree have been a murderer? "I hadn't even thought about Margaret's grandfather as a suspect."

"Could have been George or even her father Henry. He would have been eighteen in 1923," Owen said.

"You're right." According to the records I'd seen, Evelyn would have been twenty, and Margaret's father Henry would have been eighteen.

"If they really didn't approve of the relationship, the Donovans wouldn't need much extra incentive to get rid of Frank. If he planned to go to the authorities, that might have given them the extra push."

"Do you think we can ever know who's responsible?"

"There may be clues on the body, or some kind of DNA evidence sealed in the barrel."

"Would that have survived this long?" I asked.

"Hard to say. We have some pretty advanced techniques at this point, and the guys will certainly analyze everything they can."

"Tomorrow," I said. I wished in some ways I could fast-forward through the holiday so the lab would get back to work. Then again, it had been the best Christmas I'd had in years, and I didn't really want it to end.

"Tomorrow," Owen agreed. "For now, it's still a holiday. What do you have going on this evening?"

"Amal and I are making three turkeys for the Donovans and we're joining them for dinner."

"That's a lot of bird." Owen laughed.

"What are you up to?"

"Elsa is cooking a turkey too, and Dad is snoring in the recliner."

"A lot of excitement opening gifts?" I asked.

"A lot of eggnog, actually," Owen said.

"It's warming up outside, at least," I said. The temperatures had risen, and though it was still grey and dreary, the ice had finally begun to melt.

"Yep. By tomorrow, the roads should be passable. It's supposed to be back in the high fifties."

"Good. I'll see you then?" I asked.

"Definitely. Have a good night, Dahlia."

"You too." I hung up and logged off, closing my laptop.

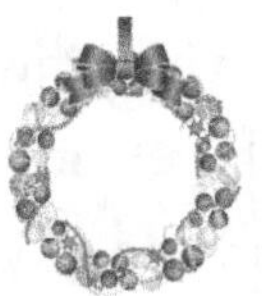

Back in the kitchen, dinner preparation was in full swing. Diantha was standing at the sink peeling potatoes, and Amal was sitting at the table removing the strings from a mountain of green beans. I sat down to help.

"Turkeys in?"

"Yep. Good thing you have two ovens," she said.

"It is." I turned to Diantha. "Did you find anything in the journals?"

She shook her head. "Not yet. There are a lot of them. I guess Evelyn kept one every year of her life."

"You're kidding." My hands paused. "Are there really more than fifty journals?"

Diantha shrugged. "Not quite, but there are a lot. I got tired of looking. She didn't always use dates, so you have to read a lot to figure out what the time frame was, and her handwriting was bananas."

"Bananas how?" Amal asked.

"Loopy and crazy."

"Like cursive?" I asked.

"Yes, but only if the cursive was written by a toddler hopped up on Froot Loops and Pepsi," Diantha said.

"Oh, well." I laughed.

"Did you figure anything else out?" Amal asked.

I shook my head. "I talked to Owen though, and we're pretty sure the man in the barrel was Frank Brown. We just aren't sure who put him there, but it seems like the motive was to stop him from going to the authorities about the illegal dealings happening at the bar downstairs. Or maybe to end his relationship with Evelyn. Or both."

"That makes sense," Amal said. "So sad, though."

"So, Aunt Dolly?" Diantha turned to look at me.

"Yes?"

"The ghost upstairs really is Mr. Brown?"

"If we ever had a ghost, then yes, I guess he'd be a likely suspect."

"And he had good reason to be looking for some attention," Amal said. "Trapped in that barrel for a hundred years."

"You've been in the Holden Suite this week. Have you heard from him at all?" I asked her.

"Not a peep," Amal said.

"Tessa promised that her cleansing would take care of it anyway," Diantha said. Our next-door neighbor and friend Tessa Damlin had blessed the room with sage a while back. I hadn't had any faith it would work, but perhaps I hadn't given our eccentric neighbor enough credit.

"Maybe it did," I allowed.

The three of us worked side by side, putting together the extensive side dishes we'd serve with the turkey, and when the turkeys were finished, we were ready to get things on the table. We quickly changed our clothes and met again in the kitchen.

"Diantha, can you go let the Donovans know dinner will be out shortly?" I'd restocked the bar cart earlier in the day and had invited the family to help themselves to drinks. I'd also put out some cheese discs and a charcuterie board to tide them over.

Diantha came back in, looking around as she walked. "They're ready when we are. Have you seen Taco?"

Alarm flared through me. Had I closed him outside and forgotten him? How had I not noticed he wasn't with me? Had I traded my most loyal companion so easily for this new family?

But my eyes found him quickly, tucked onto his dog bed in the corner of the kitchen, napping quietly with his enormous Christmas bone tucked beneath his chin.

"He's right here, Danny," I told her. "He's just exhausted from all the excitement of the last couple days, I guess."

"Oh!" Diantha crossed the space and dropped down next to Taco, petting his head and cooing at him. "He was so quiet and still, I didn't even notice him here. I got worried."

I smiled at my tired dog and turned back to the dinner preparations. "We just need some serving utensils, and we'll be all set. Are you both ready?"

"Ready," Amal said.

We carried out the extensive collection of dishes out one by one, finally returning to the table to take our seats with the family. Margaret had insisted that Christmas dinner would be an all-inclusive event, and she wouldn't hear of us eating separately. I hoped the family had gotten past their previous bickering, but was determined to enjoy the meal either way.

Chapter Fifteen

"Overdoing things just a bit, aren't we?" Emily asked as Peter's exceptionally well-dressed family stepped into the dining room. "You're not a guest on the Tonight Show or anything. It's just us."

Peter and Sabrina were dressed as if they were attending the Met gala instead of sitting at dinner in a seaside inn, but Peter's tuxedo did lend a certain air of glamour to the evening. Sabrina's red satin one-shouldered gown was gorgeous, and I wondered how she'd managed to travel without it ending up wrinkled. Even Isabelle was dressed to the nines, in a sparkly black dress with her hair pulled up and fastened with a diamond clip.

"Excuse us if we prefer to dress for an occasion," Peter said, giving his sister's loose, flowing tunic a sneer. "You could have made a bit of an effort." His eyes came to rest on her Birkenstock sandals, which she'd paired with thick yellow wool socks.

Emily didn't respond, just let out a weary sigh.

Oliver and Lily were both in party clothes, and their appearance in the dining room was accompanied by boisterous laughter as Oliver chased Lily to her seat.

"Kids," Vanessa called, entering after them. "Oh, sorry, everyone. They're so excited." Her eyes scanned the table. "Oh Dahlia, Amal... this looks amazing."

"It does," Margaret said, taking her seat at the head of the table. "It looks perfect, and I think everyone looks just lovely."

Everyone took their seats, and I glanced at Amal, who looked as uncomfortable as I felt, given the clear tension between the siblings.

For his part, Eric seemed to be able to ignore whatever issues lay between his sister and brother. He grinned widely and took a seat between his children. "Looks great. Merry Christmas, everyone."

As we passed the food and everyone served themselves, Margaret watched the proceedings with a secretive smile on her red lips. She'd dressed up a bit too, I noticed, and her cheeks looked rosier than usual above the lipstick she'd clearly applied with care.

"I got this race car set," Oliver was explaining to Diantha across the table. "And the tracks can go up the walls and over things, and you have a remote control thing like this, and the cars go super fast, and—" his tiny hands were waving through the air over his plate as he explained his gift to Diantha, and Eric caught them just before Oliver knocked over his milk.

"I'm glad you're excited about your presents," Eric said. "Try not to destroy the table."

"He always talks with his hands," Lily said, rolling her eyes.

"Only when I'm extra excited," Oliver said with a shrug.

"Well, I hope everyone got what they were wishing for today," Margaret said, pulling the attention of the rest of her family. "Having all of you here, in this place that has meant so much to me and to our family for so long is a wonderful gift to me." She gazed around the table, letting her eyes rest on each of her family members.

"I want to thank you, Dahlia, Diantha, and Amal, for the amazing efforts you put forth to make us all comfortable and happy during our stay. I know no one intended for us to be inside the entire time, but I do appreciate the grace with which you shifted plans and meals to accommodate both my family and the weather."

"Of course," I said, inclining my head and then feeling silly for having done it. Margaret was not the queen, after all. But the way she was addressing the table from its head, and her regal air, gave that impression.

"There is one more thing," Margaret said. "And I hope

you'll humor me as I explain the final Christmas gift I have for you all."

Peter actually rubbed his hands together, and exchanged a meaningful glance with his wife. Clearly, they were expecting this.

"I told you that I wanted you all to join me here this year because I wanted to discuss my final wishes for my estate," Margaret said.

"Mother, maybe not over dinner," Emily moaned. "It's so morose."

"For heaven's sake, let her speak," Peter snapped. "She's not going to keel over right here at the table."

Emily actually turned and stuck her tongue out at her brother, and Diantha and I exchanged amused glances, trying to keep our thoughts hidden.

"This is not morose," Margaret continued. "It's simply a reality that I will not be here forever."

"Margaret, are you ill?" Vanessa asked, reaching for her mother-in-law's hand.

"No, no, nothing like that," Margaret said, patting Vanessa's hand and then taking a quick bite of turkey. She chewed slowly, holding the attention of everyone at the table. Then she took a sip of her wine and turned to me. "Dahlia, the food is just amazing. Well done."

"Thank you," I said. "Amal did a lot of the cooking too."

"Well," Margaret said, looking at Amal. "Bravo to you both."

Amal did the head incline thing I'd done a moment before, and I felt slightly redeemed.

Margaret continued. "I am not a young woman. One day, I'll leave this life and it's very important to me that my legacy and my family are taken care of properly."

Peter nodded sagely.

"I care very much about all of you, and am so proud of the way you've each taken on the world, finding your own way and carving out your lives. I know that our family name, and our legacy is just as important to you all as it is to me, and I wanted to discuss this here at the Saltcliff Bed and Breakfast because this inn is a fundamental part of that legacy."

"Here here," Eric said, raising a glass.

Peter shot him an annoyed look and turned pointedly back to his mother. "Go on, Mom."

"Yes, well." Margaret cleared her throat and then smiled around the table. "Our shared love for this place and our desire for our legacy to live on are the reasons why I am transferring a significant portion of my estate to a trust for the inn."

"You're what?" Peter leapt to his feet before realizing that his reaction had been outsized for the occasion. He sat back down. "Sorry, you're doing what?" His voice was quieter, but laced with tension.

"I want to ensure that the inn continues operating, that the renovations on the bar downstairs are successful and done with quality, and I want to continue to be a small part of the place that has been so important to my family for so long," Margaret explained.

Peter shook his head. "But..."

"So you're leaving your money to a building," Emily said, her voice flat. "Figures."

Margaret's smile fell. "What does that mean?"

"Just that you've always used money to do whatever you want, never really thinking about what anyone else might want," Emily said.

"Uh, Em. That money sent you to that private school to get the degree you decided not to use," Eric pointed out. "It gave us all a good childhood, a good education."

"Thank you, Eric," Margaret said.

Emily sighed but said nothing further.

"And it's supposed to be our inheritance," Peter spit out, his face red.

Margaret stared at her oldest son. "You don't need my money, Peter. Your firm is successful. You and Sabrina live a glorious life. You have everything you ever wanted." Her pride in her son's accomplishments was clear as she spoke these words.

"We were counting on..." Peter stopped speaking, as if realizing that he was about to tell his mother he'd been eagerly anticipating her death. "We just thought..." He raked a hand through his hair. "I mean, you're still leaving us something, right?"

"Rude," Emily muttered. "Mother, should we really be discussing money at Christmas dinner?"

Margaret sighed and shook her head. "I didn't intend to discuss the details of my will. I only wished to share my plans for the trust while Dahlia and Diantha are here with us. They own the inn we all care so much for, and I wanted them to feel assured that they will have the funds they require to see to its upkeep for years to come."

"That's very generous," Diantha said.

I felt a blush climb my cheeks. I should have said something. My niece was more adept at navigating complex social situations than I was. How embarrassing. "Yes, it is. Thank you, Margaret."

"Don't go counting your dollars just yet," Peter snapped.

"Bro," Eric said, looking between me and Diantha. "Sorry, ladies."

"It's fine," I said.

"No." Peter stood again. "None of this is fine. It's not your money," he said to me, pointing at me across the table. "And it's not supposed to be. It's our money, and I need it. I was counting on it. If I don't get that money..." he trailed off, his face bright red.

"If you don't get it, then what?" Emily asked.

"We're going to declare bankruptcy," Sabrina said

softly. "Peter made some investments that didn't pan out. We've lost everything."

"Seriously?" Emily looked amused by this news.

Peter sank back down in his chair, staring into his lap.

"Dad?" Isabelle said in a small voice. "Is that true?"

"It'll be okay, honey," Sabrina said, patting her daughter's shoulder.

"Oh dear," Margaret said, her face suddenly looking drawn and much older. "Oh Peter."

"I screwed up," he said softly. "We have nothing now. I'm going to have to sell the house."

Isabelle's mouth dropped open. Peter and Sabrina had clearly been hiding the truth of their financial situation from everyone until now, waiting for Peter's inheritance to save them.

"Can you pass the cranberry sauce?" Oliver asked loudly, glancing around, oblivious to the weight of the conversation going on at the table.

"Here you go," I said, handing it to him.

"Well, there is actually one other thing," Margaret said. "I might as well just tell you all of it now." She fixed her gaze on me. "Dahlia, when I depart this earthly plane, I'd very much like to be buried in the garden out front."

Shock trickled through me. "Um. What?"

"Buried. On the property, please. With a bit of a plaque, maybe. I'll arrange for that all before I go."

Amal and I exchanged a look. "I'm not sure you can

bury people on private property inside the town," Amal said softly.

"I'll get everything taken care of, don't worry about that," Margaret said.

"Er..."

"Mom, when's the last time you had a doctor's visit?" Peter asked quietly. "Did they check everything?"

"Are you suggesting that Mom is losing her marbles?" Emily asked, grinning. She was clearly enjoying Peter's disappointment and financial revelations.

"I just wonder. This is a little out there," he pointed out.

"I am fine," Margaret snapped. "Sharp as a tack."

I believed she was. But I wasn't sure what to make of her desire to remain here at the inn as her final resting place. It was a bit unconventional, but I didn't have good reasons to decline.

"Dahlia, Diantha, we can work out all the details with my lawyers tomorrow when everyone is back from the holiday. I have a few things you'll need to sign."

"Mom, won't you reconsider?" Peter said. "We need help."

"No," Margaret said. "You don't need help, you need money, and I don't appreciate the way you are asking for it."

"I'll ask whatever way you want," he said. "Just tell me what you want me to say."

Margaret put her fork down. "Son, I am sorry that you've been irresponsible. We can talk about a loan, perhaps, but this is certainly not the time. Let's see if we can enjoy the rest of this lovely meal." Margaret looked around the table. "Please, let's talk of other things. I'm sorry my announcement wasn't quite the gift I'd imagined it to be."

The inn's finances were fine, but having a trust to ensure its future wasn't something I would turn down. I just wasn't sure we needed to plan to acquire another body when we'd finally gotten rid of the one we had.

Dinner concluded in the same awkward manner in which it had begun, with Peter fuming, Eric smiling, and Emily sneering. Once we'd each had a slice of pie, Amal, Diantha, and I retreated to the apartment, eager to be away from the strange energy the Donovan family had wrought at the table.

"Some merry Christmas," Amal said as we sank into the cushions of the couch.

"It could have been merrier," Diantha said. "I feel awful for Isabelle."

I nodded, at a loss for any words that might make my niece feel better about her friend's situation.

"She has a family that will look after her," Amal said. "And money is not the most important thing in families."

"Love is," Diantha said, looking between Amal and me.

"Right," I agreed. Taco Dog trotted over, depositing his

enormous bone on Diantha's lap and releasing a groan that sounded a little bit like agreement.

"Gross!" Diantha laughed, picking up Taco's gift and setting it onto the floor.

That night, I lay in bed a long time after the apartment and the inn had grown quiet. The gentle sounds of ice melting outside created an odd soundtrack of drips and drops, all of it overlaid with the constant rolling of the Pacific Ocean just beyond the cliffs.

Chapter Sixteen

Iwas up very early the day after Christmas, long before any of the guests or even Taco Dog were moving around.

After setting up the coffee to brew and heating the oven to bake the quiche I'd prepared once I thought it was time, I decided to head down to the basement to look at some of the books and journals that had been stored there.

The journals, most of them in identical leather-bound books, were stacked to one side. The handwriting was, as Diantha had said, difficult to read. And some of the words, even when deciphered, didn't make a lot of sense in the later years. Margaret had hinted that Evelyn had needed help toward the end of her life and might have been senile. Maybe she'd suffered from dementia, I thought.

I moved back to the other books, many of which were still packed into the boxes, since the girls had clearly given up the search once they'd found the letter they sought. I began pulling them out, trying to decide if it might make sense to donate some to the library or just find another place in the inn to put them where they might be enjoyed. I was setting aside a copy of *The Great Gatsby* when the spine of another book caught my attention. *Great Expectations*. Had there always been two copies, I wondered?

This was the book the girls had been so excited to find, but it was a second copy. The other version was upstairs on the table in front of the fire. I'd seen it there just this morning. This one was newer; the edges of the leather cover were stiff and sharp, unlike the worn corners of the book upstairs, which was soft from repeated handling.

I flipped the book open, thumbing through the pages, and was surprised when a piece of paper fell out into my lap.

Another letter? Did all copies of *Great Expectations* hold secret correspondence?

I unfolded the worn paper, reading the words with increasing excitement.

July 30, 1923

My dearest sister,

I know that you may never fully understand my actions, and for that, I will accept whatever bitterness or frustration you may feel. But in time, I believe you will come to see that I acted only out of love and duty—to you, to our family, and to the future we must protect.

It grieves me little to write that Frank is no longer a concern. He is gone now, as he ought to be, and with him, the threats he carried. There will be no more whispers in dark corners, no more fear of disgrace, nor any shadow cast upon our family's good name. All that could have jeopardized our lives and reputation has been handled.

You are safe now, Evelyn. I know you may feel sorrow, perhaps anger, and you may even question my motives. But know that I have only ever sought to protect you and to preserve your feminine dignity. No one else needs to know the truth of the matter, and I trust you will keep this between us as a matter of honor to our family.

You have always been dear to me, and I have taken these steps only to shield you from what was certain to become a greater sorrow. One day, I hope you'll under-stand the sacrifice I've made in carrying this burden.

Your loving brother,

Henry

I sat for a long moment, rereading the words.

It wasn't an outright confession, but I believed it was as close to one as we might get. I'd run it by Owen, of course, but it seemed clear to me that Henry had found out about Frank and Evelyn, known about their plans to run away, and acted to save his sister's reputation. I was less clear about whether Henry knew of Frank's plans to expose the family's illegal dealings, but the outcome was the same either way.

Margaret's father had killed Frank Brown and hidden him inside a barrel. And then he'd replaced the book where Frank and Evelyn exchanged messages, ensuring she'd find this letter instead of the last one Frank had written to her.

The thought of it—of every part of it—made me sad. Poor Margaret, who clearly believed her father and grandfather were good men, worthy of having their legacy preserved in the form of the trust she wanted to make to the inn. I doubted very much that she knew anything of their darker dealings. And she certainly wouldn't want to know her father had killed a man. Would she?

Finally, I tucked the letter back inside the book and set it aside, determined to finish sorting the others. The truth weighed on me though, and I wanted to talk through the ethics of concealing the truth from Margaret with someone wise whose opinion I trusted. Amal had planned to go home this morning if the roads were clear, so I didn't think I'd get to speak with her and didn't want to bother her on her day off. I resolved to call Owen as soon as it was late enough. Or better yet, if I could get outside, I'd pay him a visit.

I sorted through the remainder of the old books, boxing the ones I planned to donate, and then turned to Evelyn's journals. These, I thought, should be offered to the family. I could offer to ship them so they wouldn't have to travel with them. Decided, I began putting the journals into a separate box. One of them slipped out of my hands, and fell to the cement floor, opening on the way down and laying open to reveal a piece of newspaper that had been held between its pages.

Carefully, I unfolded the old newsprint, reading the headline topping the page, which was dated August 1923. "Donovan Questioned in Bootlegging Scheme."

The article detailed suspicions about George Donovan's potential involvement in the transport of illegal alcohol into the region where the inn operates.

I picked up the fallen journal and flipped through more pages, releasing several more folded articles, all of them casting the Donovan men in a less-than-upstanding light. The last one I unfolded held my attention: "Donovan Discovered Shipping Alcohol from Canada." The article quoted George Donovan, who supposedly said, "I'm simply a mariner. I live for the love of the sea. I have no idea how that devil water came to be on my boat."

It was that word—*mariner*—that got my attention.

I pulled out another of Evelyn's journals, this one holding entries from 1926, and found more newspaper articles, including one describing a distant Donovan cousin on trial for murder. The piece suggested the man was linked to some kind of organization involved in several unsavory activities up and down the coast.

Was Margaret's family involved with the Mariners? Were they possibly the original Mariners?

I collected the journals into a box, tucked it behind the laundry supplies, and then went upstairs, carrying the old worn copy of *Great Expectations* with me.

Chapter Seventeen

"Dahlia, slow down," Owen said when I'd finished explaining everything that had transpired since we'd spoken last. "You're saying the Donovan family was a part of the Mariners organization? And that Evelyn was collecting news articles linking them?"

Taco and I had gone to the police station at noon, when the ice on the streets had been mostly reduced to puddles.

"Yes, I think so. She had the letter from her brother about Frank Brown that I told you about," I said. "So she knew he'd been killed—and it sounded like Frank had been gathering evidence against the Donovans, which he was going to use to try to keep them safe once they ran away together. But with him gone, she was stuck. A woman on her own in the early twenties didn't have many choices."

Owen nodded, his green eyes sad. "That's true. So she was forced to remain at home with the people who killed her boyfriend."

"People involved in illegal activities."

"Right," Owen said, picking up an envelope on his desk. "I think there's more to it, actually."

"What do you mean?"

"The results from the lab came in just before you arrived. They found something else."

I sat up straighter, a little thrill shooting through me. "What did they find?" I expected definitive evidence of who'd put Frank Brown in that barrel.

I did not expect another mystery.

"This." Owen removed a plastic pouch from the envelope and set it on the desk in front of me. Inside the clear plastic was a rusted key on a chain.

"A key?"

"It was around his neck," Owen said, his eyes fastened to the key.

"So, obvious question..."

"We don't know. It could go to anything. The age of the key, as I'm sure you realize, means that whatever it unlocked might not even exist anymore."

"Is the shape of the key indicative of any specific type of lock?" I asked.

Owen held up the key and we both peered at it. The shaft was narrow and elongated, and the oval bow at the top bore faint engravings that were impossible to read. Time had softened the once-shiny brass, leaving it with a warm patina that spoke of years tucked away in secrecy.

"I'm not sure," he said, squinting at the key. "Could be to a safe or a padlock. Maybe something at the inn?"

"Would Frank Brown keep something that needed to be guarded by lock and key at the inn where he suspected criminal activities?"

"He might have," Owen said. "It's as good a place to start as any. He spent a lot of time there and the woman he loved lived there."

That was all true, and I didn't have any better ideas just yet. "What do you think the engraving said on the top?"

"Could be a serial number," Owen said. "I can only make out the number one."

"Actually," I said, leaning in closer and taking off my glasses, which allowed me to see detail if I held things up very close. "It could be the letter L."

"Neither gives us much of an answer." Owen put the bag down on his desk and I put my glasses back on.

"Are the Donovans staying much longer?" Owen asked.

"Until the second," I told him.

He nodded. "Everything okay having them there so long?"

I thought about the strange dinner we'd had the night

before. "Mostly, yes. Although I'll be happy when they're gone. The whole visit has turned a bit odd."

"Odd how?"

"I mean, maybe it's not odd. Maybe it's kind."

"What are we talking about, Dahlia?" Owen's smile lit his eyes and they sparkled in that way that made my skin flush.

"Well, Margaret made an announcement at Christmas dinner. She said she wants to use her estate, which would have been her children's inheritance, to create a trust for the preservation and improvement of the inn. And that she wants to be buried in the garden."

Owen let out a laugh and then covered his mouth. "Okay, yes, 'odd' fits the bill. But the trust is a good thing, right? I mean, unless you're one of her kids."

I looked away, trying to find words to articulate the discomfort that had accompanied thoughts of the trust's creation. "We haven't looked through the details yet," I said. "But I can't help thinking money tends to come with strings."

Owen's face grew serious. "It often does. But a grave plot in the garden is a pretty big string. Maybe that's all she wants."

"Maybe," I said.

"You going to have a lawyer look over the trust paperwork?"

I'd already planned to call Mr. Adams, the lawyer

who'd explained my sister's trust to me after she'd died and left me guardianship of the inn and my niece. "I definitely will." I paused, filing the trust away in my mind and focusing on the key again. "So what now?" I asked.

"Now we go hunting for a lock that's missing a key, I guess."

"What should I tell Margaret Donovan?"

Owen looked at me for a long moment. "For now? I wouldn't tell her anything. First, let's see if we can figure out exactly what there is to tell."

I returned to the inn with Owen, pleased to find it empty for the afternoon. The Donovans had clearly made the most of the good weather and were finally getting to venture out to enjoy the adorable village of Saltcliff, which was glistening and sparkling in all its post-holiday glory.

Diantha was sprawled on the floor in the living room when I invited Owen inside, working on her electronics kit.

"Hey Aunt Dolly. Hi Owen."

"Hey Danny. Whatcha doing?" Owen squatted down to get a better look and Taco took a seat at his side, leaning into him.

"I'm just going to tidy up the lobby quickly," I told them, heading back out. Since Amal was taking the day off, there were more plates and mugs from breakfast than usual, but I carried them all to the dishwasher and got it going, wiping down surfaces and setting a fresh pot of coffee to brew.

When I went back into the apartment, Owen was helping with Diantha's project, laying on his stomach on the floor beside her. Taco was at his side, and I was certain he would have been helping too if his paws could have handled the little wires they were manipulating.

For a moment I just watched them, my heart warm inside my chest as I took in the scene. This was something I'd never imagined in my own life. I knew Owen was not my husband, and Diantha was not my child. But it didn't matter - this was my family. And the love I felt for them was inexpressible. So I didn't try. I just stood quietly and soaked in the feeling of belonging somewhere, of being needed, of the joy that came with the knowledge.

"You ready to seek some locks?" Owen asked, catching me watching them and rolling to his knees and then standing up.

"What locks?" Diantha asked.

"We have a key," Owen told her. "And we don't know what it fits. But it could be something here at the inn."

"Ooh, fun," Diantha said, getting to her feet and then picking up her project and setting it on the desk inside the apartment door. "I'll help." She glanced at me, probably to see if I would decline the help. "Aunt Dolly, you okay?"

I realized, a beat too late, that tears were running down my cheeks. I hadn't intended to cry or done so consciously, but now humiliation threatened to rush in behind those tears. "I'm fine." I wiped furiously at my cheeks, pulling my glasses off as much in an effort to not see the confusion on the faces before me as to clear my eyes. "Let's look for locks."

I turned and we all headed out the apartment door, but as I did, Owen's hand found mine and he gave me a gentle squeeze as if he understood exactly what I'd been thinking.

We began the search in the laundry room in the basement, since that was where I'd found the last big secret in the inn. But there did not seem to be any safes or doors hiding anywhere else in the dim room.

"What about the other part of the basement?" Diantha asked.

"Good idea." We headed into the apartment and down the basement stairs there. Another very dim and mostly unexplored space. And another place where we didn't find any locks needing keys.

We continued the search through closets and bookshelves, finding nothing that might need a key of any sort.

"This is going nowhere," Diantha said after an hour of searching.

"You don't suppose it would be in a guest room, do you?" Owen asked.

"I doubt it, but I guess it could."

"Well, I wouldn't feel right going into those, since they're occupied," he said.

"I have to change the linens and towels anyway," I told him. "I can check while I'm in there."

Owen and Diantha exchanged a look. "If you're okay doing that," he said.

"I can help," Diantha told me. It was the first time she'd ever volunteered to help clean. Usually it took some kind of bribery or low-grade threat.

I smiled at them both. "Great. Well, I should do it before they all come back this afternoon from the village."

"I need to get back to the station anyway," Owen said. "Let me know what you find. I'll keep thinking about other things it might unlock."

"Safe deposit box?" I suggested. "Or a post office box?"

"I thought of those. Not sure if they'd still be around if that was what it opened a hundred years ago, but I'll do a bit of digging."

"I'll call you when we're through," I told him.

Owen leaned forward and gave me a quick kiss, which sent me into another furious blush.

When he was gone, Diantha smiled widely at me. "Your boyfriend really likes you, Aunt Dolly."

I didn't have an answer beyond the smile I couldn't seem to hide. The whole idea of having a boyfriend was so foreign I still hadn't wrapped my head around the idea that it could be true.

Diantha and I began upstairs, changing sheets and towels, running loads down to the laundry and poking around guest rooms in places we hadn't thought to look before in hopes of finding a lock we'd never noticed. We were finishing up in Margaret's room downstairs when the first of the guests came back to the inn.

"Hello! Anyone here?" Peter's voice was no less abrasive than usual when it came through Margaret's closed door.

I popped my head out of the door and called back. "Hello Mr. Donovan. We are just finishing up refreshing the rooms. Can I get you something?"

"The bar cart would be nice. There are no glasses and no ice. It's afternoon, isn't it?" There was a note in his voice that I supposed could have been humor, but it sounded like mildly disguised annoyance.

"Peter, it's awfully early." Sabrina's voice came down the hall.

"We're on vacation, and this scotch is paid for. With my inheritance."

I exchanged a look with my niece and then hurried out to the lobby.

Peter and Sabrina stood side by side holding their hands out to the fireplace, while Isabelle's feet could be heard heading up the stairs.

"Did you have a nice time in Saltcliff?" I asked as I arranged the bar cart and picked up the ice bucket to carry inside to fill with ice.

"We did," Sabrina said, sending me a smile. "It's so charming."

"Small," Peter said.

"That's part of the charm," his wife answered.

I hurried down to the laundry where the ice machine was and filled the bucket, trying not to allow my irritation with Peter's manner to affect me. He was a guest, and their stay was nearly over, I reminded myself.

As I replaced the ice bucket and put out fresh glasses, Peter moved to my side to pick one up and fill it.

"I suppose you've been feeling pretty merry after Mother's news last night?"

I stopped moving and looked at him. "Not really," I said, sensing several layers to his comment but unable to pull them apart adequately.

"Well, if you think you're getting a penny of my inheritance, you might want to think again."

"Peter!" Sabrina cried in a high voice. "I'm so sorry, Dahlia, don't listen to him."

"I'd listen," he said softly. "Because I'll fight you for it. And I'll win."

"I have no intention of fighting for any money," I told him. "We haven't even seen the agreement," I pointed out.

He snorted in a very unpleasant way and turned around, swigging the twelve-year scotch I'd put out. I made a mental note to replace it with the cheaper stuff when this bottle was empty.

"Excuse me," I told the couple, returning to finish helping Diantha with Margaret's room. "Find anything?" I asked quietly.

"Nope." Diantha handed me a pile of towels.

"Actually," I said, handing them back. "If you could run these down and see to the laundry, I need to get the afternoon tea ready to go and call Owen to let him know this was a bust."

Diantha let out a dramatic sigh. Now that the treasure hunt was over, she was back to being put-upon to help, I guessed. The trials and tribulations of teens, I thought, shaking my head as I locked up Margaret's room and headed back through the lobby to the apartment kitchen.

Inside, I collected a plate of holiday cookies and set the gingerbread loaf cake in to bake. It would take an hour. In the meantime, I called Owen.

Chapter Eighteen

"No luck, huh?" Owen said when he answered, anticipating my news.

"None."

"Well, that makes one of us," he said in an amused tone.

"What luck have you had?" I dropped into one of the chairs at the kitchen table and Taco stood and walked over, only to drop into a heap at my feet. I petted his soft head while I listened to Owen explain.

"The best thing about a tiny town that doesn't rush into any kind of innovation or technological advancement is that lots of things here are old," he began.

I waited, knowing there was going to be much more, but that Owen was enjoying the wind up to his revelation.

"And that's good news for us because according to Mr. Thornton, the bank manager, any safe deposits that are on record as having an owner have not had the locks changed unless the owner has requested it. They renew locks when the boxes change hands."

"So if it's a safe deposit key, it'll still open the box?" I asked.

"Exactly."

"Well that's good news. If it's a safe deposit key."

"But if it is a safe deposit key, we can't open the box without a warrant."

"Oh. That sounds time consuming. But maybe it's a key to a PO Box?"

"Well, the postmaster says the boxes in most of the local post offices don't have keys. They are cubbies that have to be accessed from the back office by an employee and he doesn't know if it's always been that way or not."

"So probably not a post office box then."

"At least not now. If that's what it is, whatever was in it is probably lost to time."

I glanced at the timer on the oven. With Amal out today, it was probably a bad idea for me to leave the inn again. The Donovans would all be returning and they might need something. At least I wasn't on the hook for dinner tonight.

"I don't think I can get out again today to visit the bank. At least not in the next few hours," I said. "Do you think Mr. Thornton might be able to meet with us tomorrow to look at the key?"

"I figured you'd say that. I'm going to visit him today just to see if what we have is a safe deposit key to his bank. If it is, I'll get to work on the affidavit for the warrant and see if I can get it through a judge in the next day or two."

"Will that be hard during the holidays?"

Owen made a clucking noise. "I'm not gonna lie—it's not ideal. But I have an in with Judge Braverman, and I'm not above calling in the favor to get this fast tracked."

"Okay, well, I guess the first step is finding out if it's even a safe deposit box key."

"So I'll call you as soon as I know," Owen said.

"Okay. Talk to you soon." I hung up, anxiety spooling within me. I wanted answers immediately. The idea of waiting for a warrant to find out what was in the box was frustrating—but since we didn't even know if it was a key to a box at the bank yet, I'd just have to wait.

I tidied some of the leftover wrap and ribbon from the previous morning and then removed the gingerbread cake from the oven and set it to cool.

Taco was watching me from his bed with big, sad eyes.

"I know," I told him, guilt dancing a tango inside me with the anxiety already there. "It's been too cold and busy for walks, and that's not fair to you, is it?"

Taco let out a long, low grumble. Agreement, I thought. I dropped to sit at his side and petted him, focusing all my attention on my sweet, loyal best friend.

"I haven't forgotten you, Taco," I assured him. "We've

gotten busier, you and me. We've had more people come into our lives, haven't we?" Those soft amber eyes met mine, full of love and patience. "But it's always the two of us against the world, right?"

Another low chuff.

"Tomorrow when Amal is back, we'll get time for a lunchtime walk, okay?"

The big eyes fell closed as I stroked my friend's side. He was endlessly patient and always forgiving. If only humans were so easy to understand and get along with.

I popped the gingerbread cake out of its pan and drizzled on the icing, which ran down the sides. It was perhaps a bit too hot to ice, but when I'd made the cake before, Diantha had preferred to spread on her own icing, so I put the rest in a ramekin and set it next to the cake on the platter with a little cheese knife for spreading. I carried both out to the lobby, where most of the family was now relaxing by the fire.

"Ready for some afternoon snacks?" I asked, setting down the cake. "I have some cookies and gingerbread cake, and the coffee should be hot and there's water here for tea," I told the group. Margaret was missing from the gathered family, but as I turned to take my post at the reception desk, she called out from the dining room.

"Dahlia dear, will you join me for a bit?"

I stepped near to see a stack of papers in front of her on the table. "Oh, sure."

"I thought we might go through what my lawyer's put together for us now."

"I did want to bring my own lawyer to look," I told her.

She waved a dismissive hand. "That can come later. For now, we'll just review the basics. You don't need to sign anything today."

I took a seat at her side, my stomach uneasy. I could feel Peter's attention on us, and his stare was like hot daggers into my back.

"You'll see here that the trust will be established with this amount." Margaret's pink-painted fingernail underlined an amount of money that was difficult for me to fathom. The inn had a bank account, but this number made our operating account look like petty cash.

"Oh," I said, unsure how one acknowledged such a number appropriately.

"And here you can see that the trust will be administered by the trustees." Margaret's finger underlined her own name and Diantha's.

"Diantha is a trustee?"

"Well, since the inn will technically be hers, yes. But of course, I'll handle oversight until she is of age."

Diantha would not officially take possession of the inn until she was twenty-two. That was nearly a decade away. If I was understanding the terms correctly, this trust would be operated completely by Margaret Donovan until then, and it had responsibility over all aspects of the inn's operation.

"Here you can see the establishment of the Donovan museum to one side of the lobby," Margaret said. "I'm having the plans drawn up back home right now."

"Oh," I managed.

"And I'll appoint a manager for the museum to ensure the Donovan heritage is correctly represented to visitors to the museum and guests at the inn."

"Correctly represented?" I asked.

Margaret lifted her head and the friendly old eyes gazed into mine, becoming suddenly clear and hard. "I think you might understand that there are those who would seek to malign the name of a family as long respected in the town of Saltcliff as ours." One of her drawn-on eyebrows rose as she waited for my response.

"Oh?" I said, hoping she might say a bit more. It was suddenly apparent that Margaret might know more about her father and grandfather's dealings than she'd let on.

She let out an irritated sigh. "There are ancient rumors that need to be put to rest for once and for all. Rumors that tarnish the accomplishments of the Donovan family and besmirch the reputation of the very founders of this town. I won't have it."

"I see." She did know. I wondered if she knew about Frank Brown too.

Margaret's face softened again. "I know you'll want to

help me ensure the town doesn't forget what the Donovans have done for them," she went on as my phone buzzed in my pocket.

I slipped it out as Margaret continued narrating the contents of the pages before us, glancing at two texts from Owen.

Owen: The key does not fit a box at the Saltcliff Bank and Trust.

My hopes fell.

Owen: But it is a match for the Daring Cove Valley Bank. I'm working on the affidavit for the warrant now and have already been in touch with the judge. He'll expedite the approval.

I pushed down my urge to react with excitement and focused on the papers before me.

Margaret was still describing her family's contributions to Saltcliff, and though I knew it was rude, I interrupted her.

"Mrs. Donovan, forgive me. I have a few things to attend to. Would you happen to have a copy of this I can give to my lawyer?"

"It's already in your email, dear," she said, gathering the papers back together into a stack.

"Great. I'll have him take a look and get back to you."

"I'd love to have this all signed before I depart," she

said. Her smile was sweet, but there was a hint of malice in her words. I was beginning to realize that the Donovan family had a long history of manipulation and strong-arming people to get their desired outcomes. Maybe the apple hadn't fallen far from the tree.

"Of course," I said, turning to head back into the lobby.

"Pleased with your share of my inheritance?" Peter called from where he practically sprawled in an armchair by the fire.

A glance at the scotch bottle told me he was at least four drinks in.

Eric, who sat beside him, looked between us. "Dahlia, I'm so sorry."

"Don't apologize for me!" Peter sputtered.

"Someone needs to," Emily said.

"It's fine," I told them, busying myself at the desk. I typed out a response to Owen.

Me: That's fantastic.

Me: Mrs. Donovan just walked me through the trust she wants to establish. It gives her full control of any changes at the inn until Danny comes of age in 10 years.

Owen: How very convenient.

Me: I'm certain she knows of her family's darker history.

Owen: Well at least we don't have to worry about her being surprised when she finds out her daddy put someone in a barrel.

Me: Right. There is that.

Chapter Nineteen

Diantha and Isabelle had gone out to the village together, and as I returned to the registration desk to double check the upcoming week's reservations and activate the confirmation messages to go out, they tumbled in the inn's front door, laughing.

"Hello girls, did you have a nice time?"

Diantha's face was lit with a bright smile as she turned to me, her cheeks pink. "We had so much fun. We visited with Valerie at the bakery and then I showed Isabelle Tabitha's shop and the stuff I'm selling there, and we went down to the water for a while."

"There are so many dogs down there!" Isabelle laughed. "Do you ever take Taco to the beach?"

At the mention of his name, Taco leaped to his feet, hopeful as ever.

"Sometimes," I said. "I've been too busy to take him lately, I'm afraid."

Diantha and Isabelle exchanged a look. "Can we take him?" Isabelle asked.

"Honey, you just got back. It's cold outside, maybe take a breather?" Sabrina rose from her seat on the couch where she'd been reading a novel.

"She's not old and frail," Peter snapped. "Let her go run around."

"Would that be okay?" Diantha asked me, glancing at Taco, who was practically quivering with excitement.

"Sure," I said, knowing my dog needed some exercise that I hadn't given him lately. Diantha would look after him. And Taco would look after her. "Don't forget the bags," I said, handing her a little dongle to put on the leash that contained disposal bags.

Isabelle had a quick chat with her mother, which I assumed ended in permission, because the girls were gone almost as quickly as they'd arrived. I felt slightly happier, knowing that Taco was out running around for a bit. I hadn't been a good dog owner in the past week, between the inn and the weather.

I worked for a few more moments, focused on the screen before me, when Margaret approached.

"Dahlia," she said softly. "Has there been any progress you've heard about on the unfortunate gentleman discovered in the club downstairs? I've been wondering about it."

I was certainly not going to tell her about the key. Not until we had figured out exactly what it led to. But she already knew it was most likely Frank Brown, her aunt's paramour.

"Still nothing one hundred percent definitive," I told her. "But the lab does believe the man has been in the barrel since the twenties. And the discovery of the ring with your aunt's initials seems to confirm—taken together with the letter mentioning a ring—that it must be Frank Brown."

Margaret nodded sagely. "So sad. For him and for Auntie Evelyn. She must have loved him all her life, maybe that's why she could never find anyone else."

Perhaps, I mused, she was heartbroken at her own family's betrayal and decided she could never trust anyone at all. But I kept that to myself.

"Do you have any idea who might have done it? What are the police saying?" Margaret asked, her lips tightening as she waited for my answer.

"I'm not sure they would share that information with me, even if they knew," I said. She didn't need to know that I frequently helped the Saltcliff detective with investigations. Or that I was romantically involved with him.

"Of course. It's just... you know..." She looked up at me with an assessing gaze. "I would hate to see old rumors reignited through this discovery."

"Old rumors?" I asked.

She knew. I decided that she certainly knew her family might have been involved. Or she suspected it.

Margaret sniffed. "Oh, it's nothing. Just the worries of an old woman," she waved a hand and turned, heading back to sit by the fire.

"What's wrong, Mom? Worried the past might not stay where it belongs?" Emily asked, her voice a heated taunt.

"I don't know what you're talking about, Emily." Margaret picked up the newspaper and lifted it between them.

"Of course not." Emily's tone was bitter.

So it seemed perhaps knowledge of the family's history was less of a secret than I'd presumed.

The family departed for their dinner plans at six, and Diantha and Taco and I headed into the apartment for our own quiet evening.

"Aunt Dolly?" Diantha asked, looking up from her crocheting as we watched a documentary on the origins of various winter holidays.

"Yes?" I was working on my own project, a hat made from the leftover Qiviut wool I used for Owen's scarf.

"Do you ever wish we had a big family? Like the Donovans?" I could see the wistful longing in my niece's eyes when she asked this, and I imagined a large holiday gathering with cousins and aunts and uncles. It wasn't something I'd had, either.

"I don't," I said honestly. "But I do see the appeal."

"I wish we had more family," she said. "Isabelle has more cousins on her mother's side, too."

I smiled, understanding Diantha's longing tone. "Family can be wonderful. But it can be complicated too," I reminded her. "When you're very close to someone, it's easy to believe they should understand you without you having to explain things. And just because you are related by blood doesn't mean you'll agree about things on moral or philosophical levels. You're still individuals."

Diantha's nose scrunched up and she smiled. "I know you're probably right. It's just a nice idea."

"It is."

That night I went to bed, torn between the desire to give my niece everything she could ever want just because I loved to see her happy and wanting to preserve the close intimacy of this tiny family I'd only just found.

Chapter Twenty

When I awoke in the very early hours of the morning to bake the blueberry crumble coffee cake and egg cups I'd planned, I had a text from Owen that must have arrived while I was asleep.

Owen: Braverman said he'd sign the warrant today. Stay tuned.

I didn't know exactly what kind of favor Owen had done for this judge, but it must have been something big for the judge to act so quickly over his holidays to sign a warrant for a historical case.

Either way, I was glad to know there was a chance we might get some real answers about what had happened in Saltcliff back in the Prohibition era, and just how involved the Donovans may have been.

We already had what amounted to a confession from Henry Donovan to the murder of Frank Brown. But a clear motive was hard to suss out through the haze of a hundred years.

Taco greeted me as I stepped out of my bedroom, having spent the night guarding Diantha. His tail wagged so hard as he said hello that his entire body seemed to sway back and forth, and his paws tapped as he danced on the hardwood floor.

"Good morning, boy. Yes, I love you too."

Taco's head bounced up and down in a motion that I knew in a less well-trained dog would have been a full-blown jump.

"Let's go find some breakfast, shall we?"

My dog brooked no arguments with the plan and danced ahead of me into the kitchen, nosing at his bowl in case I'd forgotten where it was. Once he had a full bowl, he ate happily, and so quickly I still didn't understand how he managed not to choke.

As he stepped outside into the still-cold morning, I glanced around the garden. The ice was gone, and there were only a few white patches left here and there, spots where the snow was especially tenacious (or just places that didn't get much sunlight during the day.) There was a bracing sea breeze coming in off the Pacific, and the scent of brine mingled with pine in that uniquely comforting smell I now identified as specific to California's north central coast.

"We need to get breakfast ready, Taco Dog," I told him as he came back in, smiling broadly at me with his trusting eyes wide. "And I promise there will be a w-a-l-k today, okay?"

Taco was a better speller than many would suspect, and he bucked again at the mention of his favorite activity.

"I haven't seen my friends in a little while, either."

I turned to the sink and washed my hands and then got started on the morning's offerings for the Donovans. While I baked, the sun spread its first rays over the front of the inn, the light trickling into the backyard and eventually edging down to kiss the dark water spread out to the horizon, turning it a deep iridescent blue.

Just after seven-thirty, I carried the hot muffins and egg bites out to the lobby to set them on the side table where we served breakfast. Amal greeted me from the desk.

"How was your day off?" I asked her.

"It was lovely. I spoke with my mother and my sister for a few hours and then did a little shopping."

I didn't know much about Amal's life outside her work at the inn. It was easy to forget she had a whole family and home elsewhere. I tended to think of her as "ours."

"Do they live nearby?" I asked her.

Amal shook her head. "Not at all. They're in India.

Mom lived here when she was young, but she went back home in the eighties, and my sister went with her."

That made me sad for some reason. "So no family close?"

Amal tilted her head and smiled softly at me. "I have you and Danny, remember?"

I smiled back. "You do. And we're lucky for it."

"What did I miss?" she asked, angling her head to indicate the still-quiet guest rooms.

I filled her in on my belief that Margaret was well aware of her family's less-savory past activities and about the trust she was using to try to keep that past suppressed.

"Wouldn't it be easier for her to just ask you not to publicize it?"

"It would," I agreed. "But I guess to people like the Donovans, money talks."

"It's not far off from just paying you to keep the secret," Amal said. "Just feels less icky, I guess."

"I don't know." I shuffled through a pile of mail on the desk that needed sorting. "The trust feels kind of icky. Especially the part about turning the garden into a graveyard."

"Yeah. You're right."

A door down the hall opened, and Emily appeared, her gray curls a wild mass atop her head.

"Good morning," she called, her ever-present knitting bag slung over her shoulder.

"How did you sleep?" I asked.

"Just fine," she said. "Ooh, these look good." She'd discovered breakfast.

Soon, there was a whole smattering of Donovans around the lobby, and Amal set off to begin changing linens.

Owen called just after ten, and I went to let Amal know I was going to step out for a bit.

"You're going to the bank?"

"Owen's got the warrant to open the safe deposit box," I said. I had to stop myself from gushing as excitement at finding out what the box contained roared through me.

"Well, you'd better go then," Amal said. "But I want all the details."

"Of course."

An hour later, Owen and I were at the Daring Cove Valley Bank, presenting the warrant and the key to the manager there, Elise Bayberry.

"You know, it's actually a bit of a relief," she told us as she walked us back to the wall of boxes inside the bank's vault. "Most of our boxes have been updated with more secure locks, but our policy requires us to leave any of the prepaid older boxes untouched."

"This box was prepaid?" Owen asked.

"Oh yes, in the twenties. They had a set fee back then that you could pay to essentially 'own' the box forever. We don't really do that anymore."

I could see why not.

"Here we are." Elise fit the key we'd given her into the old lock and then put a second key into a second lock. She turned both, opening the little door and revealing a metal handle just inside. She pulled, sliding out a long metal box. "I'll set you up over here to view the contents. Will you be taking everything with you, Detective Sanderson?"

"Yes," Owen said. "It will all be entered into evidence in the Frank Brown homicide case."

"Of course," she said. "You can just leave the box and the key on the table then when you're done."

"I'll need to retain the key, actually," Owen said. "Until the investigation is closed."

"Oh, well, sure. Then you can just bring it back when it's all over."

Owen nodded his agreement, and Elise left us alone in a small room and closed the door.

"Ready for the moment of truth?" Owen asked me.

"I suppose," I said. "It's possible the box is empty."

"Let's find out," Owen said, flipping up the lid of the box. It groaned as it opened and lay flat to reveal a pile of documents inside, along with another ledger like the ones at the inn.

Owen flipped open the book.

"Dates and locations," he murmured, pointing. "Destinations listed here, and origins here. I think the Donovans were involved in a lot more than selling illegal alcohol."

I looked at the book myself. He was right. There was a full accounting of what seemed to be smuggling operations up and down the coast. The names of ships and contacts were listed, along with amounts paid to the captains, presumably to stay quiet about whatever they were transporting.

"Look at this," Owen said, flipping to another page. The words at the top read "Loyalty Insurance."

"What is loyalty insurance?" I asked.

Owen's finger traced down the column which listed the name of apparent city officials. "Judge Sherman Hilliard. Mayor Damon Pratt. Councilman Arthur Berns."

"Bribes," I guessed.

"That's one way to keep people loyal, I suppose," Owen said.

The box also contained a check register with George's signature next to payments made to the listed city officials, and the initials F.B. beside the signature where it said "paid."

"Frank Brown," I said, pointing to the initials. "Henry signed off and Frank made the payments."

"He was the bookkeeper, so I suppose that makes sense."

Owen looked up, catching my eye. "I think this is all we need, Dahlia. It's pretty clear from these documents that George Donovan and probably his son, Henry, were engaged in quite a few unsavory activities during Prohibition. Frank knew all about them and intended to go to the authorities with this evidence."

"So they killed him and put him in a barrel."

"Looks like. And I would have fingered George for it, but the letter Henry left Evelyn makes it pretty clear he was the one who handled the situation. Whether he did it because his dad told him to is something we'll probably never know."

"He thought he was protecting the family," I said.

"In some ways, I guess he was."

We sorted through the other papers and photographs in the box. There were several of Frank and Evelyn, a few receipts that made little sense out of context, a stack of letters from Evelyn Donovan, and one other document, brittle with age and folded in half.

"What is this?" Owen unfolded it.

"A birth certificate?" The form was unmistakable. "But whose?"

"Lyle Stevens?" Owen glanced up at me, shaking his head.

"Owen." I pointed down farther on the page. "Look at the parents' names."

"Adeline Stevens and...George Donovan." Owen and I exchanged a wide-eyed look.

"George Donovan had a love child?" I wondered suddenly if the secrets Margaret was so intent on keeping had less to do with the connections her family had to the Mariners and more to do with the existence of another branch of the Donovan family.

"Looks like it," Owen said. "Well, that's unexpected."

I stood still for a moment, thinking. "Do you think we should try to find out what happened to Lyle Stevens?"

Owen was tucking the items back together and putting them inside a plastic evidence bag. "I'm not sure it will change anything. This investigation can be closed once I submit all the evidence and file my report. Unfortunately, having a child with a woman who isn't your wife isn't really a crime."

"Right, but..." As someone with very little family, I couldn't help feeling like I'd want to know if my father had other children. "Would it be okay if I dug around a little bit?"

Owen stopped moving and gazed at me. "Sure, I guess. But why?"

How did I explain the strange ping in my heart? "I just feel like maybe the other Donovans would want to know if they have more family."

"I'm not sure it's our place to tell them."

I'd have to think more about that.

"I'll have the guys run a search back at the station, okay?"

"I'd appreciate that," I told him.

"Let's head out."

We left the bank together, settling into Owen's car and heading back to Saltcliff on the Sea. Owen dropped me off at the inn, promising to be in touch about any discoveries about Lyle Stevens.

Chapter Twenty-One

I was back at the inn by the afternoon and shared what we'd learned with Amal and Diantha.

"So the case is closed?" Amal asked. "Does that mean we can get back to construction downstairs?"

"It does," I told her. "But the men won't return to work until after New Year's either way."

I also told them about the birth certificate we'd discovered. "Danny, I'm telling you what we learned, but I also don't want you to mention it to Isabelle. This type of thing is delicate within families, and it's not our place to inform anyone of it."

"But wouldn't you want to know if you had distant relatives somewhere?" Diantha asked.

"I think I would," I said. "But with a family like the Donovans, there may be other concerns."

"Money," Amal said, wrapping her hand around the coffee cup that sat before her on the kitchen table.

"Exactly," I said. "Plus, I have a feeling Margaret already knows. So if she hasn't told the rest of her family, it's not our place to do it."

"I don't know how you can resist looking for them anyway," Diantha said. "Lyle Stevens. Did you Google him?"

"Of course," I admitted. "But there are many of them. Owen is running a search as a favor, but we aren't going to do anything with the information, even if he comes up with something, okay?"

Reluctantly, Diantha agreed.

That afternoon, Taco and I went for the walk I'd promised him, turning up the snow-washed Main Street of Nutmeg and wandering past the familiar shop windows, all dressed up for the holidays.

Abbey's shop, Tidepool Books, had a collection of holiday romances in the window along with cozy mysteries and cookbooks, all featuring bright red and green covers. I caught Abbey's eye through the window and waved.

"Dahlia, hi!" Abbey came to the door to greet us. "Hello, Taco."

She petted Taco's head as we paused in front of the shop.

"I'm so glad the snow is gone," she said. "It was a fun change, but I much prefer seeing people out and about."

"It does feel more like Saltcliff without the snow," I agreed.

"Do you have plans for New Year's?" she asked.

"The Donovans will still be here, so I'm on party-hosting duty that night," I told her. The Donovans had planned to stay in after a late dinner out but were expecting champagne service to ring in the new year.

"Well, that's no fun," Abbey said.

I shrugged. "It will be fine." I'd never really celebrated New Year's in the past, anyway.

"Well, I think we should have an after New Year's party, then. I'd be happy to host everyone at my house."

"That sounds fun," I told her.

"Good, we'll do it on the second," she said. "I'll invite everyone. And we can toast the new year early so no one has to stay up until midnight if they don't want to."

I laughed, feeling oddly relieved, since I didn't usually stay up anywhere near that late.

"Enjoy your walk," Abbey called, heading back inside as Taco and I progressed up the sidewalk.

The scent of cinnamon, coffee, and chocolate floated

on the air as I wandered past Beachside Bakes and Tidal Beans. Taco greeted everyone we passed with a gleefully wet nose and happy paws.

"Being inside was a lot for these guys," Tessa Damlin said, sneaking up beside me with Arthur the greyhound at her side.

"Oh! Hello!" I turned with a hand over my heart, working to recover. I had a highly tuned startle response.

"Sorry, didn't mean to scare you."

I shook my head. "No, you didn't. Not really."

Together we turned down Ginger and headed back toward the inn and Tessa's house next door.

"Well, it's turned into a beautiful week," she said.

I agreed, taking a deep breath of the afternoon air and gazing up into the bright blue sky.

I waved goodbye to my neighbor and returned to the inn through the back door, feeling lighter now that the snow was gone and the mystery of the body in the barrel had been put to rest.

But the call I got from Owen once I was inside stirred things right back up.

Chapter Twenty-Two

"**I** knew I shouldn't search that name for you," he said when I picked up the phone.

"What do you mean? Why not?"

Owen sighed on the other end of the line, and I removed Taco's leash from his collar. He trotted off to get water as I sank into a kitchen chair.

"I was worried that digging into the identity of Lyle Stevens might upset the Donovans. Now I'm worried it might upset you."

"What? Why would it upset me?"

"Because Lyle Stevens had two children. One of them was Adrienne Stevens. She married a man named Derrick Vale."

"Derrick Vale is my father's name."

"Exactly."

Shock bolted through me as I processed this information, and I found it hard to find words to ask the questions racing one by one through my mind.

"Dahlia. Are you still there?" Owen's voice was laced with concern.

"Still here. Yes." I wasn't sure what to say. I'd just realized that this meant Daisy and I were actually related to the family I'd been hosting this holiday season. The family staying in the inn was my family. And Diantha's.

"Are you okay?"

"I'm fine," I answered automatically.

"Do you want more information? I have it, but I'm kind of worried about you right now. I don't want to overload you."

"Yes please," I said, still not feeling quite right.

"Adrienne's brother was David Stevens. Your uncle. Did you know him?"

I shook my head, and then realized Owen couldn't see me. "No. We never met Mom's family."

"He didn't have children," Owen said, and I recognized the past tense he used to describe him.

"So he's gone too?"

"Unfortunately, yes. Died six years ago."

"And their parents?" I'd never met my grandparents on my mother's side, and my parents had been killed in a car crash when Daisy and I were five. We'd been raised by Dad's mother.

"Gone in the eighties."

"So Daisy and I..."

"Are the last living relatives of George's illegitimate child, Lyle Stevens. Sorry. Were. You and Danny are now." Owen's voice was soft, careful.

"Okay. Thanks." I hung up, realizing only after I'd done so that it had been rude. But I had too much to process to hold the phone to my ear at the same time.

For long moments I sat at the table in the dimming kitchen, letting the shocking information sink in as the sun dropped below the horizon outside.

"Aunt Dolly?" Diantha peeked her head around the corner, concern on her face. "You okay?"

"Oh. Yes." I stood abruptly, realizing that I'd been sitting still for an indeterminate amount of time. "I'm fine."

"Ookay," she said, drawing out the word. "You look kind of... not okay."

"I'm fine," I told her. "I just... well, I have received some news."

Diantha stepped to my side and looked up at me, and I realized in that moment how very young she really was. Did it make sense to tell her this? Would it upset her?

Processing this kind of thought was difficult. I understood facts and information on its face, but it was harder to predict the effect that certain words would have on other people—people I cared deeply about.

"You're scaring me, Aunt Dolly."

I forced a laugh. "No, no. Don't be scared. I'm just

trying to decide how best to share what I just learned. Want to sit down?"

"Not really."

Just as Diantha sank into a seat, a worried look on her face, a knock came at the door that separated the apartment from the lobby of the inn.

"Wait here," I said, rushing to answer the door. I wasn't sure how I'd face Margaret, knowing that she might have known all this time of our connection.

But I needn't have worried. I pulled open the door to find Owen there, a concerned expression on his face.

"You hung up on me."

"I'm sorry," I said, finally feeling more like myself. "I didn't mean to, I just needed to think for a moment."

The worry in Owen's eyes slid away as he smiled. "You're a fascinating woman, Dahlia."

"Most people don't think that's a good thing," I said.

Owen slipped an arm around me and hugged me. "I think it's great."

"Well, I was just about to tell Danny," I said, releasing him and stepping back inside, closing the door behind him. "Join me?"

"Should I?"

I lifted a shoulder. "I can probably use the help."

Owen actually wrung his hands, a movement I found charming. "Well, if you want me to be there."

"Come on."

"Hey Danny," Owen said, stepping into the kitchen.

"Should we get a snack?" I asked, moving to the refrigerator.

"Aunt Dolly, no! Just tell me the thing. I'm dying." Diantha nearly shouted.

"You're not dying."

"It's an expression."

I sat down between Owen and Diantha. "Owen and I found some information about the case in the basement today. And it connects to you and me."

Diantha shook her head. "What?"

Owen nodded at me encouragingly and I explained that we'd found ledgers conclusively tying the Donovans to criminal activity in the twenties.

"What does that have to do with me?" Diantha asked, looking between us. "I'm so confused."

"Tell her the other part," Owen suggested.

"I was going to. I just wanted to give her context," I explained.

"Oh. My. Gosh." Diantha said, her cheeks reddening.

"Okay. I'm getting there," I said. Then I told her about the birth certificate, and about the family connection we had to the inn and to the Donovan family.

"Wait," Diantha said in a breathy voice. "So you're saying Isabelle and me are... we're cousins?"

"I think so," Owen said.

"Yes, that would be right," I told her.

Diantha sprung up off her chair and danced around the kitchen. "That's amazing!" Then she sat back down. "But, I mean. Isn't that kind of a coincidence? That Mom bought this place that her family actually built?"

"Maybe it isn't a coincidence," Owen said.

I stared at him. I hadn't really thought about that part of it. How did my sister just happen to buy an inn that had belonged to our ancestors?

"Do you think Margaret knows about all of it?" I asked.

Owen shrugged. "There's only one way to find out."

A half hour later, I sat in the lobby in front of the fire, Diantha at my side and Margaret in the armchair I now thought of as hers.

"Do you have a few moments?" I asked her.

Margaret put down the book she held and smiled at us. "Of course."

"Well," I started, "I wanted to ask about how the inn was sold to my sister."

Diantha leaned forward. "My mom. Daisy Vale."

Margaret smiled at the mention of Daisy's name. "I knew your mother," she said, nodding at Diantha. Then she looked at me. "I'm not sure I know what you mean when you say, 'how the inn was sold.'" She spread her hands on her lap and then looked up at me. "We drew up some paperwork and she paid for it, and then it was hers."

I swallowed down annoyance at the assumption that I was asking for information about how property sales worked.

"I guess I meant...how did Daisy find out about the inn being for sale?"

Margaret shook her head. "Well, it wasn't for sale. Not really."

"Then how did she buy it?" Diantha asked.

"She asked if she could," Margaret said, leaning back as if that would be the end of the conversation.

"She asked you?" I asked.

"No, no. I had a manager running the inn back then."

The short answers were frustrating me. "Could you use more words to explain how this happened?"

Margaret chuckled. "More words?"

"Mrs. Donovan," Diantha said. "My Aunt Dolly is good at puzzles. And she just figured out that we are all related. By blood. And we want to know if my mother knew that."

Margaret's eyes registered surprise, but it passed quickly, and she glanced around the lobby to see if anyone else had heard Diantha's explanation. Amal had headed downstairs to attend to laundry when Diantha and I had first come out to talk, and no one else was around. "I guess we have a lot to discuss," she said, looking between us.

"Did my sister know?" I repeated. "When she came to buy the inn?"

"Not when she first arrived," she said. "But eventually. And I saw an opportunity."

"An opportunity? What do you mean?" Diantha sounded as frustrated as I felt.

Margaret sighed. "As you both know, I have three children."

Diantha and I nodded, trying to be patient.

"Peter is hopeless with money—constantly betting on things that don't pan out. He's been in debt since he was a teenager, and I've bailed him out more times than I can count. Emily is bitter for whatever reasons she's chosen—she thinks money is a tool people use to repress each other, and she thinks our money is dirty anyway, since it may have had somewhat nefarious origins. And Eric? He's happy. He's built his own life and has never once asked me for a dollar. He lives outside the cage the rest of my family seemed to inhabit. A cage built on wealth, but also on greed.

"I knew I'd have to either sell the inn and divide the proceeds between my children or leave it to them together. There is no way the three of them would have been able to agree on how to run the place, and I'm certain they would have sold it themselves, giving up any claim the Donovan family had on our history or our legacy.

"And then there was Daisy. And you, of course, Dahlia. The only two remaining descendants of my grandfather's third child. The one we weren't supposed to know about."

"How *did* you know about him?" I asked, unable to contain my curiosity.

"Aunt Evelyn knew. And she told me when I was a little girl. She told me everything—how her brother killed her boyfriend, how my grandfather essentially founded a criminal operation to smuggle alcohol and other contraband during Prohibition, and how he fathered an illegitimate child." Margaret smiled softly and shook her head. "The rest of the family disregarded her, and my mother and father told me she was 'touched.'" She looked at Diantha. "That's a term they used for people who were crazy, dear."

Diantha nodded.

"But she told me stories about our family, and I listened. And when I was grown, I did a bit of digging to find out whether they were true. I didn't know about poor Frank down in the basement, of course. But I didn't doubt that my father had killed him. Or that Grandfather had another child he supported secretly. Once I had inherited the estate, it was easy enough to follow the money trail and prove it was true. He wouldn't acknowledge Adeline or

Lyle publicly, of course, but he supported them financially all their lives."

That made sense. I let out a deep breath I'd been holding, and some of my tension dissipated with it.

"And I made a point of monitoring you and your sister," she went on, looking at me. "Daisy visited the inn because of a postcard I created for her."

"What?" I shook my head; not sure I heard her right.

"I would have sent you one too, dear, but you were so busy, and my sources told me Daisy was between jobs. A bit lost, maybe."

"What did the postcard say?"

"It invited her to the inn, to an all-expenses paid weekend stay in Saltcliff."

"And she came?" Diantha said.

Margaret nodded. "And fell in love with the town, as I'd hoped she would. During her stay, I suggested the manager let slip that we were seeking a buyer, and Daisy showed interest. That was when I met with her."

"You met with my mom?" Diantha asked, a note in her voice that belied just how desperate she was for any glimpse of the mother she'd loved so much and lost so young.

"I did. And I told her how we were related and promised to sell her the inn at a very discounted price, with certain specific contingencies."

"Like what?" I asked.

"Like not mentioning the connection to anyone."

"Why not?" Diantha asked.

Margaret shrugged. "There would be no way to protect my family's legacy in the minds of the people of Saltcliff if they knew my grandfather was a philanderer. And a bootlegger."

I supposed I understood that logic. That explained why Daisy hadn't told me we had family. "She never told me," I said, hoping to show this woman that my sister held up her end of the deal.

"I figured," Margaret said. Then she sighed and leaned back into the chair, looking much smaller and much older suddenly. "But to be truthful... the secrets are wearing on me."

"Why does it all still have to be secret?" Diantha asked the old woman, and I knew she wanted to embrace this new family she'd suddenly been granted. I also knew she'd keep the secret if Margaret asked her to, just as her mother had.

Margaret looked between us with sad eyes. Then she shook her head. "I don't even know anymore. Maybe it doesn't."

We sat quietly in front of the fire for long moments, each of us in our own thoughts.

Then the front door of the inn opened, and the rest of the Donovan family came in with a rush of conversation and laughter. Isabelle came straight to Diantha and flopped down at her side.

"We went to the aquarium. Have you been?"

I watched Diantha's face as she looked at the girl she now knew was her family. She pressed her lips tightly together and then smiled, nodding. "Yeah, I've been there a few times. It's great, right?"

"So amazing," Isabelle said, oblivious to Diantha's struggle. "The octopus was my absolute favorite. Wait, no. The otters!"

"The otters!" Lily clambered onto her cousin's lap as the adults hung up their coats and came in to warm up by the fire.

"It was pretty great," Eric said, kissing his mother's cheek. "Mom, you should have come."

Even Peter smiled as he came to sit by the fire.

"We should let you enjoy your family," I said, rising.

"Or maybe," Margaret said, looking at me and holding my gaze for a long moment. "Maybe you should stay and enjoy them too."

"Mother," Emily said in her usual annoyed tone. "I'm sure they have things to attend to."

I gazed at my cousin, wondering where the bitterness Margaret gave name to had come from. Despite her dislike of money, she seemed accustomed to dismissing 'the help.'

It was strange, looking from face to face, identifying characteristics we all shared. These people shared my blood, my history. It was a feeling I'd never experienced before.

"May I?" Margaret asked me, her eyes moving from mine to Diantha's. My niece turned to me. "Please?"

"Sure," I said. It wouldn't hurt anything now, I didn't think.

"I have something to tell you all," Margaret said. "Please sit down."

Chapter Twenty-Three

As Margaret finished her story, the rest of the Donovan family gazed at Diantha and at me, their faces holding varied expressions from happiness to confusion to something that looked a bit like anger from Peter.

"Why didn't we know about any of this?" Peter asked.

"I thought I was protecting my family," Margaret said. "Your family. You."

"Maybe you should have kept the secret," Peter said. "Now we've just got more outstretched hands, waiting for you to keel over."

Sabrina gasped and Eric put a comforting arm over his mother's shoulder.

"I think you're the only one waiting hopefully for my death, Peter," Margaret said, rising. "And I'd like to make it perfectly clear right now that my will does not change in any way just because this news is now public. Diantha and Dahlia will have a very comfortable life here running our family's inn, thanks to the trust."

I hadn't signed the trust yet, and really hadn't intended to, but I wondered if the news of our relationship being less secret might allow us to adapt the portions of the agreement that gave Margaret full control. Or the part about the graveyard in the garden.

"You are each named as well, of course," she went on, addressing her children. "But I would much prefer if we focused ourselves on enjoying the time we have left together instead of planning for any of our unfortunate departures. We are a family. And we should celebrate that."

Isabelle rushed to Diantha and grabbed both her hands. "Danny! We're cousins!"

"I know!" Diantha lifted her hands and threw them around Isabelle's neck, hugging her tightly. My heart squeezed inside my chest. It seemed Diantha had gotten her Christmas wish.

Amal, who'd come upstairs during Margaret's explanation to her family stepped close to my side now.

"Are you okay?" she asked.

I nodded. "I am, yeah. I'm great."

As the family settled a bit and conversations went on around us, I sat with Margaret once more. I still had a question.

"Margaret?"

"Yes dear?"

"When we first looked over the trust, you mentioned certain rumors about your family that you wanted to keep hidden. What did you mean exactly? Us?"

Margaret's smile fell. "I don't know anymore," she said. "I wanted to keep my family's name clean, I suppose. I didn't want anyone talking about my grandfather's less praiseworthy doings."

"But those were the things that led to the family you are now," I pointed out.

She nodded. "I really am tired of keeping secrets, Dahlia. And if you'd like, we can revisit the portions of the trust that were created for that purpose alone."

I agreed, and after a little more conversation, I went back to attending to the business at hand.

For the rest of the Donovan's visit to Saltcliff, the atmosphere was dramatically different than it had been for the first part. We ate together, both in the dining room and out in town, and Diantha and I both accepted invitations from our cousins to go for walks, or to go shopping in town in an effort to get to know one another. Even Emily proved to be friendly once she'd gotten past the initial shock, and we found ourselves talking about knitting and crocheting as we showed one another the projects we were each working on.

Emily's project, as it turned out, was an enormous blanket to cover her king-sized bed.

Peter wasn't entirely friendly, but his bitterness seemed to dissipate as he accepted us and saw how excited his daughter was to have a cousin close in age.

By the time the Donovans left Saltcliff, I'd signed a new trust—one that gave Margaret and I equal control until Diantha came of age—and Diantha had accepted an invitation to visit Isabelle and her parents in Newport Beach over the summer, in the house Margaret's generosity would allow them to keep. And Margaret had already planned her next visit to Saltcliff for the spring. She'd also agreed to a memorial plaque in place of an actual burial site in the inn's front garden.

On January second, the inn felt like a different place entirely.

"It's so quiet," Amal said.

"It is," I agreed, pouring myself a cup of coffee in the empty lobby as the sun shone through the windows, signaling that our cold snap was coming to an end.

"Your family was a lot of fun," she said, grinning as she called the Donovans my family.

"They were," I said. It felt a bit like a dream, thinking about all the cousins I suddenly had. It was as if the world had expanded around me, as if my little island of security and warmth had doubled in size and grown in population and the number of people I cared about in the world had done the same.

"I'm so happy for you and Danny," Amal said.

Diantha emerged from the apartment and sank down to bury her hands in Taco's ruff. "I miss them," she moaned.

"I know," I said. "I do too."

"Well, hopefully it won't interfere with your normal duties," Amal said brightly. "Because you have school today, Danny, and we have guests checking in this afternoon."

I smiled, happy that life was about to return to normal, but also aware that everything about my place here at the inn had changed. More than ever before, I felt I had a place I belonged. Saltcliff on the Sea really was my home. (And Taco Dog's too, of course!)

Dahlia's Gingerbread Loaf Cake

Dahlia's Gingerbread Loaf Cake (with high altitude adjustments)

Ingredients:

- ☐ 1/2 cup dark brown sugar (reduce by 1 tablespoon at high altitude)
- ☐ 1/2 cup butter, softened
- ☐ 2/3 cup molasses
- ☐ 1 large egg
- ☐ 2 cups all-purpose flour
- ☐ 1 teaspoon baking soda (3/4 teaspoon for high altitude)
- ☐ 1 teaspoon ground ginger
- ☐ 1 teaspoon ground cinnamon
- ☐ 1/2 teaspoon nutmeg
- ☐ 1/4 teaspoon ground cloves

☐ 1 teaspoon salt

☐ 1/8 teaspoon freshly ground black pepper

☐ 3/4 cup hot water (reduce water to 2/3 cup at high altitude)

Instructions:

- Preheat the oven to 325°F and coat an 9 x 5 inch loaf pan with nonstick cooking spray. (If baking at high altitude, raise the oven temperature to 350.)
- Cream the butter and brown sugar together and stir in the molasses and egg until well blended.
- Sift in the flour, baking soda, cinnamon, ginger, nutmeg, cloves, black pepper and salt; stir until completely combined. Stir in the hot water until the batter is smooth.
- Transfer the batter to the prepared baking pan. Bake for 50-55 minutes or until a toothpick inserted in the center comes out clean. (For high altitude, time may be closer to 40 minutes).

Spiced Brown Sugar Icing

Spiced Brown Sugar Icing

Ingredients:

- [ ] 1/4 cup butter (softened)
- [ ] 1/2 cup dark brown sugar (packed)
- [ ] 2 tablespoons milk (you may need slightly more depending on your preferred consistency)
- [ ] 1 cup powdered sugar (sifted)
- [ ] 1/4 teaspoon ground cinnamon
- [ ] 1/8 teaspoon ground ginger (optional for a little extra spice)
- [ ] Pinch of salt (to balance the sweetness)

Instructions:

- Melt the butter and brown sugar together in a small saucepan over medium heat. Stir until the sugar is dissolved, then remove from heat and allow it to cool slightly.
- Add milk: Once slightly cooled, stir in the milk until the mixture is smooth.
- Add powdered sugar and spices: Gradually whisk in the powdered sugar, cinnamon, and ginger (if using) until the icing is smooth and reaches your desired consistency. Add a bit more milk if the icing is too thick.
- Spread over the cake: Pour or spread the icing over the loaf once it's completely cool. The icing will set as it cools, creating a smooth, slightly crackly top.
- This icing will add a nice, warm sweetness that enhances the flavors in the loaf without overpowering it. Enjoy!

More Nancy

The Saltcliff Mystery Series:

Book 1: Keeled Over at the Cliffside

What happens when Gilmore Girls meets Murder, She Wrote? You get Dahlia Vale and snarky Diantha along with Taco Dog solving murders in the Saltcliff Mystery series! Follow along as Dahlia builds her community and family, and solves mysteries along the way. You'll love the small town vibe, B&B setting, and romantic sub-plot in this cozy culinary series!

The Windthorne Witches Series:

Book 1: All Hallows Hex

Wine, Witches, and all kinds of Weird... What's a midlife witch to do when her peaceful magical life is upended by murder?

In the cozy wine town of Moonridge, California, magic flows as freely as the local vintages—and for the Windthorne sisters, it's the key to their family's success. Filled with sisterhood, humor, and heart, this series is the perfect mix of cozy mystery and paranormal intrigue. If you love witchy vibes, midlife magic, and small-town charm, join the Windthorne witches as they face down ancient secrets, dark forces, and the challenges of everyday life—one spell at a time.

Other Books - Steamy Small Town Romance written as Delancey Stewart

The Wilcox Wombats Series:

Book 1: The Wedding Winger

Ready for some ha ha with your hockey? The Wilcox Wombats bring the camaraderie and sense of found family you're looking for, along with snort-laughs and swoons. The first book features a star winger planning for his future, but caught up in the past. When his high school touch (the smart girl who always thought he was just a dumb jock) moves back next door, he knows he's in trouble. Grab it here!

The Kasper Ridge Series:

Free Prequel: Only a Summer

Book 1: Only a Fling

Read the Kasper Ridge Series to get your fill of small town steam with plenty of humor! Former fighter pilots share deep bonds and plenty of inside jokes. Step into their world as they join together to help renovate the Kasper Ridge Resort, a dilapidated mountain property in Colorado, left as an inheritance to Ghost, one of their own. But the inheritance also comes with a treasure hunt! Each book follows a different couple but each story builds another link in the hunt, so read them in order! Start with Only a Summer, which is free! Then pick up Only a Fling here.

The Singletree Series:

Book 1: Happily Ever His

What happens when the totally normal sister of a movie starlet meets her ultimate movie star crush, only to find out he is dating her famous sister? But it gets a bit more complicated than that.

Tess's sister has brought movie hottie Ryan home for her grandmother's 90th birthday to show the world how quickly she could move on after her very public divorce. The relationship is just for show... but Tess doesn't know that at first. And Gran? Is a video gaming, weed smoking, take-no-prisoners firecracker who tells it like it is. Toss in a lovesick chicken, and you're on your way to understanding what kind of series Singletree promises to be. Plan to laugh. Pick up book 1 here!

The MR. MATCH Series:

Free Prequel: Scoring a Soulmate

Book 1: Scoring the Keeper's Sister

If you enjoy a side of sports with your sexy men, and want both wrapped up in a hilarious package, then you're going to love Mr. Match. Soccer star and genius Max Winchell has discovered the formula for love and built a dating app around it. Though he keeps his identity secret, he convinces all his teammates to try it... and one after another, they fall in love. First up? Fernando "the fire" Fuerte, who shares an enemies-to-lovers romance with PR rep Erica, who happens to be his teammates twin sister. Taboo, forced proximity, and tons of witty banter up the steam in this one! Get it here!

The KINGS GROVE Series:

Book 1: When We Let Go

Coming right up, a bit of Sequoia mountain steam mixed with small town swoon! Head to Kings Grove for quirky side characters, emotional love stories, happy ever afters, and a cast you'll want to make your neighbors. Book 1 features Maddie returning to her childhood home, only to be swept off her feet by a handsome and potentially dangerous stranger. These books are steamy and engaging, with a touch of humor. Read book 1 here!

***THE GIRLFRIENDS OF GOTHAM* Series:**

Book 1: Men and Martinis

Head to to the dot-com heyday of NYC - the late 1990s! Join Natalie Pepper as she makes her way in the big city in this Carrie Bradshaw meets Bridesmaids coming of age story. Meet the girlfriends here!

The Digital Dating Series (with Marika Ray):

Book 1: Texting with the Enemy

Looking for sweet romance with a romcom kick? That's what you get when Delancey and Marika Ray team up! In this series starter, Elle is texting a guy she isn't sure she likes, but boy does he give good text. The only problem? She's actually texting her boss since "the guy" gave her his buddy's number instead of his own. Now she's falling slowly in love with the perfect guy and can't figure out why he doesn't seem perfect in person... Needless to say, hilarity ensues. Pick it up here!